A Gathering of Stories: Valentine's Day

Praise for other Stories Rule Press anthologies

Imaginative and just a delightful read.

I absolutely LOVE this collection!!!

Other Stories Rule Press anthologies

Thriller Digest 2022: Hunted

Space Opera Digest 2022: Have Ship, Will Travel

Christmas Romance Digest 2021: Home for the Holidays

Space Opera Digest 2021: Fight or Flight

Contents

A Gathering of Stories: Valentine's Day

By

BONNIE ELIZABETH
C. A. ROWLAND
JOHANNA ROTHMAN
M.D. POSEY
TAMI VELDURA

Stories Rule Press

Murder for Valentine's Day

By Bonnie Elizabeth

CARLTON RIVER CASTLE WASN'T EXACTLY a castle. More like a big Federalist building along the side of a huge gorge that rarely held any water, so the whole river thing in the name wasn't any more truth in advertising than the name "Castle". Still, it was about as romantic as I got for my short break from work.

It was my honeymoon, in theory. Aiden had gotten time off from his job in IT. He worked remotely so we could live not far outside Louisville where I worked at the FBI office. I was riding a desk because my tongue had gotten the better of me one too many times. I wasn't exactly a senior officer and the only reason I had a job was because everyone agreed that the mayor of the last town I'd been posted in was built like a pregnant moose and had the brains of a sand flea. They just held their tongues rather than telling him that in person.

The mayor wanted me fired. My boss went to bat and I got a slight demotion and moved to a Kentucky office. Last year it was Pikeville. This year I was in Louisville, working my way back up the ladder, so to speak, although the station head wanted me at a desk for the foreseeable future. Who knew what would come out of my mouth, though I tried to tell myself that I had learned my lesson.

Devoted Aiden had followed me wherever I got posted, working remotely at his job, and trying to be a calming influence to my less than calm persona. And now we were legal. Man and wife. He'd get the government bennies if I got killed in action, not that I was likely to see anything sitting at a desk outside of Louisville.

Feeling generous, my boss allowed me the week of Valentine's Day off to go on honeymoon with Aiden. Or maybe Aiden had called him and sweet-talked him. Aiden was good at things like that. He'd have made a great diplomat, but Aiden preferred money to influence and power, although arguably the money he made gave him influence and power.

I let Aiden pick a romantic place for us to vacation. He'd chosen a spot at the edge of the Appalachians, not so far in as to remind me of my year in Pikeville hell, but close enough to have some level of beauty. I'd seen the images of Carlton River Castle online. It did look pretty even if it didn't look like a Castle.

Red brick walls and white columns lined the front. A wing stuck out on one side, more modern hotel than cute old house looking, with a weird square tower at the far end, probably the most castle-like thing. The odd wing was still red brick and white trim but it looked somehow both newer in that the brick was plainer, and older in that they'd been laid in patterns that made it look like some of the bricks had started to sink down, as if it had been there for ages. Either way, it didn't match the look of the front.

The white columns in the front held up a long wooden porch with rockers of the sort you might see at Cracker Barrel, all painted white. We parked in one of the spaces to the side and got out to check in.

No valets or porters greeted us. There were other cars already there. I noted the makes and models, all nice cars. The price of the Castle wasn't bad, though it was cheaper than say a weekend at the Kentucky Castle in Versailles. Really, when Aiden had talked about it, at first, I had thought that's where we were going. Disappointingly, it was not our destination. Of course, in hindsight, it would have been a calmer vacation.

We crossed the parking lot and came to a rather narrow path that led to the front porch, where we walked up three wooden steps. The breeze outside was chilly enough that I crossed my arms. The area smelled of damp leaves and rancid oil, the latter seeming to come from the not-quite-a castle.

I wrinkled my nose and made a face.

"If it's bad, we can cut it short and find something else," Aiden said. It wasn't as if we couldn't afford it. Aiden might like money, but he was also a saver and if something went wrong, he wasn't averse to tossing it all in and going elsewhere. But he'd try first. I mean just because it stank outside didn't mean it was a bad place.

"Good beds and good food," I said quietly, smiling at him.

Aiden beamed his thousand-watt smile at me. He really was too handsome for someone like me. I was short and rather round, the figure described as a fireplug. He wasn't terribly tall, an inch or so shy of six-foot but he was rather rangy, the sort of thin that comes naturally and not from working out. His blonde hair was rather messed, but in a sexy way, and his brown eyes were sharp and missed nothing, though they were hidden behind thick lenses.

I thought he was terribly handsome. For some reason, Aiden found me beautiful though I tended to be more non-descript than anything. A good thing for my job. I could watch folks and no one noticed. I mean, if I weren't stuck behind a desk where people would notice me, if only because of the desk.

"Good beds especially," he whispered to me as he opened the heavy-looking wood door. It was one of two but both had handles and both were dark black, contrasting with the red brick and white columns.

Walking inside, there was a huge coffee colored desk to the left of the doorway. It took up what had probably once been an old parlor. Old-fashioned cubby holes that could hold letters or keys lined the space behind the desk, though I noted a laptop computer sitting on the desk itself. A bell waited to be rung.

The door closed behind us with a swish and from somewhere I heard a computerized ding-dong, probably to let someone know people had come inside.

The building smelled of that old building smell, the faintest hint of damp and old wood that was doing its best not to rot. I heard creaks and groans from all around us as if a hundred little elves were waking to help us check in.

Rather than an elf, a very tall woman, several inches taller than Aiden, walked into the entry and looked at us.

"We're the Baxters," Aiden said. "Checking in."

The woman nodded at us, looking down at the computer. She typed away at it, not once looking at us again.

"You said honeymoon?" she asked looking up at us. Her nose was as long as her frame, but a bit too wide for the horsey shape of her face. At some point in history, she'd have been described as a handsome woman. Now she just looked rather outdated, her eyes a faded blue. Her style of clothing, dark jeans and a casual blue sweater did nothing to change her look, though it did make her a bit more modern, rather than like a spinster out of a painting.

"I did," Aiden said smiling.

"Congratulations." The word was said flatly as if she didn't care. In fact, I suspected I'd get more emotion if we'd said someone had just died. Perhaps even a smile had that happened.

"Thank you." As always Aiden was far more gracious than I was.

I bit back my sarcastic comments.

"I put you in the Rose Room," she said. "All rooms are named after flowers. I like flowers."

Aiden smiled and nodded and while he filled out some paperwork that included giving her our license plate, presumably so that she wouldn't tow our car, she stared at us, her eyes chilly. If she were an actress, she'd get good work in horror movies.

"I'm Maude," the woman said. "I run the place. I have one elevator. I ask that you not use it late at night as it can keep the guests in the rooms closest awake. I serve breakfast from seven to nine in the morning and that's included. You'll have a menu in your room before bed so you know if it's to your liking. I don't do substitutions."

Maude led us around a corner. Stairs led down to the hallway. Just beyond, in the curve of the stairs was a silver door. The elevator.

"Your room is on the second floor. All the best rooms are. Faces the gorge in the back. People like the view. There's a balcony if you want to sit out there. No hot tub, which disappoints some people. Those rooms are more expensive and they were booked before you booked yours. If you want specialty things here, pays to book early," Maude said. She looked accusingly at Aiden as if our lack of a hot tub was all his fault for not thinking appropriately ahead for our honeymoon.

Never mind that I wasn't interested in sitting in a hot tub on a balcony in February in the Appalachians. Might be pretty or romantic for some. I had to pinch back a shiver just thinking about it.

"We're good," Aiden said.

Maude pressed the up button for the elevator. I noticed there was a down as well. The place had a basement. There might even be rooms down there if it were a walkout. We were at the edge of a hill.

"Do you run this place all on your own?" Aiden asked as we got into the elevator. It was larger than I expected, though rather plain. Dark, near black floors, shiny and clean. The walls were also shiny black with lighter wood paneling halfway up.

"I own it," Maude said. "I have a girl come in to help at breakfast sometimes and two people who clean rooms.

I do everything else, mostly."

She sighed.

"It sounds like a lot of work," I said.

Maude stared at me as if I'd insulted her. I tried to work out what could possibly be insulting about the words I'd said. I'd wanted to commiserate with her. I was so used to putting my foot in my mouth that it didn't even occur to me until later that this was a strange reaction.

"I was engaged when I bought the place," Maude said. "Each year I miss him more."

She didn't look at me as she talked.

We rode in awkward silence the rest of the way, even Aiden not certain how to approach further commentary.

When we got to our room, Maude inserted the metal key into the lock and then turned. I noticed that our key was linked to a large plastic shape with the flower pictured on it, along with a number, though not the name of the hotel. I preferred the key cards that told no one anything about us, but this would have to do.

Maude let us go first, though neither of us had our suitcases. The room was larger than expected with a big four poster bed in dark wood. A flat screen TV sat across from it. Near the sliding door was a pair of club chairs and little table. The bathroom had a large shower with a seat and a big jetted tub next to it. The two sinks gave two people plenty of space. This might not be a honeymoon suite with a hot tub but it was nicer than most places I stayed.

"Very nice," Aiden said.

Maude nodded and then turned leaving us with the parting comment about breakfast.

"I'll see you at breakfast. It ends at nine sharp, so don't come down a minute before expecting to get anything."

"Thanks!" Aiden said.

"Wow. She was something," I said after the door was closed and we started poking around our digs. The room had a slightly musty smell.

"She seems lonely," Aiden said picking up something I had missed.

I shrugged. I let myself fall back against the bed, enjoying the feel of the mattress, the soft spring of the top and then the firmer lower level. I was going to sleep well that night.

THE NEXT MORNING, I WOKE early as was my habit. Aiden was still sleeping but I got up and pulled on a coat and went to sit on the balcony. Chill air slithered up through my night gown along my legs, raising goose flesh. Coffee would have been perfect out there. White frost lined the limbs of trees that climbed the hillside across the way and far below, in the bottom of what might have once been a river gorge, I saw what I thought was ice, though I could have been wrong.

Pink sun rose on the horizon, off to my left. In summer the rooms would be warm with the southern exposure. In the early spring, the air was still too cool for the warmth to make too much difference.

When I could stand the cold no longer, I went back inside. Aiden had gotten up, probably feeling me moving around next to him and deciding it was morning. We were well within the seven to nine time frame for breakfast.

"Happy Valentine's Day!" he said, nuzzling my neck. He gave me a small box of chocolates. Just four pieces. There was probably a larger box at home.

"Is this breakfast?" I giggled slightly.

"Nah. I say we have eggs and a Swedish pancake," Aiden said. "Let's go. You can have eggs, right?"

I nodded. I had celiac. I wasn't always good about avoiding gluten. In my job, the way I ate, it was nearly impossible, although being stuck on the desk, it had become easier. I could bring food or order in from places that I trusted would get me true gluten free items. I wasn't certain about here. Eggs could have cross contamination. Fortunately, my system wasn't so clean that I'd get sick from a little cross contamination.

"Let's try it," I said. I put on my clothing and quickly prepared to go downstairs. I was wide awake after a wonderful night's sleep. The bed had been amazing and not just for sleep.

"I want one of those mattresses," I said as we headed for the stairs. I would have taken the elevator, but Maude's comment about not using the elevator unless we had to echoed in my mind. It hadn't sounded noisy to me, but I hadn't been there that long.

"Maybe for your birthday?" Aiden smiled. My birthday was in May. Almost halfway to Christmas. He'd do it, too. And it would be wonderful.

"We need to find out what type they are," I said.

"Don't they have tags?" Aiden asked. "You know the ones that you can get arrested for removing?"

I laughed. It was an ongoing joke. Was it a federal crime that they would call me in to investigate or a local crime? Who knew?

The dining room was across the entry from the reception desk. It was long and narrow and had several long tables with benches. Two other people were at the end of one of the long tables. Aiden and I went for the end of a second one, but Maude came out and directed us to sit at the same table as the first couple.

"That way if not everyone comes down, I'm not cleaning a bunch of spots. I know where you all sat."

I gave her a tight smiled and nodded. Not exactly a romantic Valentine's breakfast. The couple next to us didn't look exactly thrilled to have us there. They were older than Aiden and I, but clearly there for a romantic weekend. She had a frilly sweater on and jeans. The lines on her face rose up, telling me she was a smiler, normally.

"How's the breakfast?" Aiden asked after Maude had taken our orders for two coffees and one orange juice for Aiden.

I avoided eating and drinking things that might have anything gluten in them. Juice was normally safe, but now and then something could set me off. I didn't want to ask her about what brand, though in a hotel I might have. Something about Maude put me off.

"Tasty," the man said after a moment. His face looked pale, like he was battling something. Upon a closer look, the woman looked a bit on the pale side, too.

He put his fork down, halfway through the pancake and eggs.

"I just don't seem to have my usual appetite. We'll probably cut our stay short and head home. I haven't been well," he said.

"I think I'm getting it, too," the woman said. She'd not touched her eggs but was working on the pancake, smeared with jelly.

I had said Maude didn't need to bring me one and she reminded me that there were no changes. I either had all the breakfast or none. I shrugged and figured it would just sit there going to waste, but if that's what she wanted, who was I to say otherwise.

"How long have you been staying?" Aiden asked again.

I leaned away, not wanting to talk to two sick people. I hated getting sick. And if it was at all gastrointestinal, with my celiac, I'd take longer recovering.

"We got here two days ago," the man said. "It's quite lovely. Supposed to be a nice Valentine's Day vacation, but..."

He shook his head as he trailed off.

The woman said very little.

A younger couple came in. The woman stumbled a bit walking into the room. They sat down at our table, not having to be told to sit with us.

"She's very weird about making us all sit together," the girl said sitting next to me. I noticed she looked a bit pale, too. There were dark circles under eyes. I wondered what was going around and was beginning to reconsider eating breakfast in the breakfast room if everyone was sick.

Maude came out and got their drink orders while delivering coffee to Aiden and me, along with his juice. She was back moments later with our breakfasts. I pushed the pancake aside, glad it was at least on its own plate.

"The pancake is the best," the girl said. "She makes them every morning no matter what else. The eggs tend to be a bit overdone." She looked around at the last, worried that Maude would overhear.

"Can't have gluten," I said.

The girl looked like she was about to say something, but Maude came out with their breakfasts. The eggs, as the girl had said, were slightly overdone. I picked at the eggs and sipped my coffee. After I ate what I could of the eggs, I poked at the fruit cup which held a few slices of melon and a single purple grape.

The girl said nothing, but quicky took a bite of eggs and nodded at Maude. Then she started putting syrup on her thin pancake. Aiden had taken a few bites of his but was mostly working on the eggs. I wanted to ask him what was wrong with it. For once I managed to keep my mouth shut in front of the others.

The older couple finished and shuffled off. Another couple came in while Maude was cleaning the end of the table. They took seats next to the young couple. Perhaps the next couple would sit on our other side.

Aiden pushed his coffee back and nodded at me. He was ready to leave, the pancake only partially eaten. I'd finished the eggs, though they weren't all that good. I needed the protein for the morning. We planned to hike.

The girl sitting next to me fell backwards off the bench.

I leaped to my feet, as much as I could given that there was a long bench. Aiden was already standing. The young man with the girl was sitting there, looking stunned. The new people appeared perplexed, not sure what was going on.

Leaning down, I checked for a pulse. Faint. She was barely breathing.

"Call an ambulance!" I shouted.

Maude came in. "What's the fuss?"

"We have a person down," I yelled. "Call 911."

"I'm sure there's no need," Maude said coming around the table.

I glanced up at Aiden. He had his phone out and was calling. Fortunately, we had bars for that. The reception up here wasn't great, but it wasn't non-existent.

"She's probably just tired," Maude said standing over us.

"Her pulse is faint. She's barely breathing," I said. "And no idea if she hit her head falling backwards."

"Well, that's not my fault!" Maude said. "I think we can just bring her up to her room and let her rest. No sense getting her all upset if she's not feeling well. Lots of folks have been poorly around here."

I glared at her. "This could be a medical emergency."

"Are you a doctor?" Maude put her hands on her hips.

"No…" I started.

"See. I worked in healthcare. This girl just needs to rest upstairs. I'll help take her up to her room. She was probably kept awake for too long by people taking the elevator too often." Maude glared at me as if I'd used the elevator more than the one time she'd taken us and then again when we brought our bags in perhaps an hour later. We'd taken time to check out the mattress for things other than sleeping.

I glared at her. "Don't move her. This could be a crime scene."

"What are you talking about?" Maude snapped. Her hands her back on her hips. She rose to her full height towering over where I knelt next to the girl.

"FBI," I said. I didn't have my wallet, my badge. That was up in the room. It would have felt good to pull it out and let her know I did have some authority here. "And until I hear from the EMTs that this is an ordinary virus that she's reacting too, I'm saying this room is a potential crime scene."

"You can't!" Maude said. "The locals have to call you in. And I'm calling them now, to make an official complaint about you!"

She marched off. I couldn't care less. My boss wouldn't care, not when he heard what she was hoping to do to this girl who was clearly unconscious. I touched her shoulder trying to wake her. Her pulse remained thin, almost non-existent, worrying me. This was no normal virus.

I remembered how pale the older people were. The new people who had come in and sat down also looked a little peaked. Everyone who was here ought to be tested. Aiden and I ought to be tested.

My stomach felt knotted, but in the normal way it did when I was working, not from eating something bad. Perhaps Maude wasn't just a bad cook. Maybe she didn't clean the kitchen. She'd talked about being alone and not liking it.

That would need to be looked into. I would be asking the EMTs how often they came up here, how often people went to the hospital after staying here.

Time stretched. The pulse beneath my fingers faded to nothing. I started CPR. Aiden knew it as well and he came over to offer rescue breathing between the pumping I gave the girl's chest. I had a vague awareness of other people standing around, more people than should have been there, but I knew the bed and breakfast was nearly full. Aiden had said so when he'd attempted to get reservations.

Finally, I heard the sirens of an ambulance. Instead of EMTs, the police came in.

"Her!" Maude shouted at them, pointing at me. "She's trying to murder that poor girl! Stop her!"

"She's doing CPR, ma'am," the officer said. I appreciated the tired tone of his voice, as if he were used to working with hysterical people. Probably was.

"The girl doesn't need it! She fell. And was a little sick. Just needed to go upstairs and have a lie down, but this woman is going to break her ribs all to make me look bad! She's been trouble since she checked in!" Maude was yelling.

The officer knelt down. I backed off while he felt for a pulse.

He nodded at me. I went back to CPR.

"What are you doing?!" Maude screamed at him. "Stop her!"

"This girl doesn't have a pulse when she stops," the officer said. "If she wasn't doing CPR, I would be."

He said something into the radio. Perhaps warning the EMTs what was going on.

The young man who had been with her slumped down next to Aiden, his head at an awkward angle. The police officer went over to him and felt for a pulse. He laid the young man on the floor and started working on him.

Definitely something going on in this place.

It wasn't long before I heard more sirens. Maude was still screaming about leaving people alone and that she knew they just needed to go upstairs and rest. Fortunately, the police ignored her.

I kept working, feeling my arms tiring but knowing I had to keep going, especially because the young man this girl was with needed the assistance of the two officers who had arrived first.

Finally, the EMTs arrived. One immediately noted what was happening and called for another bus. I moved back when one started to take over where I was. I gave him my mental notes on how long I'd been doing CPR. He took over without a word. I stepped back.

Maude's voice slowly came into focus.

She was still upset that no one was leaving these poor children alone.

"They aren't children," I snapped getting up and going over to her. "In fact, your insistence upon leaving them alone makes me wonder what you might know about their collapse."

Maude stared at me.

"You horrible woman! How dare you even think that I could hurt someone staying at my bed and breakfast! These people are my family. I have no one else!"

I waited, not moving, just watching her face. There was something else, something Maude didn't want to say.

"We'll have to test the food you've been serving. All of it, to make sure there isn't some sort of contamination," I went on, watching her carefully.

Her throat moved as she swallowed hard. A tell. She wasn't comfortable with that. We were definitely testing the food, preferably the food the young woman and young man who had collapsed were eating.

More police arrived and I told one of them to take samples of the food the two were eating. The other went into the kitchen to take samples from there, lest the contamination have happened between kitchen and dining room.

The officer who went into the kitchen was young, barely out of school, his skin so smooth it made me think of a baby. I wondered if he had to shave at all. His fair hair suggested that even when he did shave, it wasn't very noticeable. He was taller than I was and broadly built, though, solid. He wouldn't get a lot of crap about his baby face, not with that build. Or maybe he'd bulked up after getting crap about his baby face.

"You local?" I asked. Anyone looking that young, probably was.

"Grew up here," he said. "Never seen anything like this."

"How long has Maude run this place?" I asked.

"Heard you was a Fed? You taking over?" he asked me, staring. Not a fool then.

"Fed, yes. Not taking over. Not unless there's a reason. I'm nosey when I'm stuck in a place someone might have tried to kill me."

He understood that.

"Maude's been here for about a decade. She inherited the place from her father. He built the wing off to the side. Thought he was some bigwig in the mines, but that went bust and he nearly lost the place. The only reason he didn't was he died conveniently and she inherited. She and her husband paid the taxes taking in boarders and vacationers and gradually built this place up."

"What happened to her husband?"

"He got sick of her," the kid said. "Living in town now with another one of the nurses from the urgent care clinic. She's older than Maude, so it's not like he was looking for a younger woman. Just someone he could talk to, I think."

The kid seemed sympathetic to the husband.

"Must be hard to run a place like this, alone."

"Heard that if it wasn't so popular, she would have let it go. Had a few offers from corporations about taking it on, but she says this is all she has," the kid said. "Although she'll probably sell soon enough. Heard she had some sort of invasive cancer. Can't run a place like this if you're sick."

"No." It was interesting that Maude had cancer. She looked strong and fit. Of course, looks could be deceiving.

I had a feeling Maude was good at pushing through. She seemed like the type. As a nurse, she might even have a good sense of what she could and could not expect from her illness. She'd also have a good sense about poison.

"She was a nurse before running this place, yeah?" I asked.

The kid nodded. "She was nicer then, I heard. I didn't go to the clinic where she worked, but people really liked her. It was only when she started running this place that she got kind of weird. And mean when her husband left. Everyone was always surprised that people came back the way she sort of insisted on having things a certain way."

"Like everyone eating at the same table as if we knew each other," I threw in.

"Heard about that," the kid said. "Yeah. That would put me off. I mean this is advertised as a romantic destination and she insists people be friendly together. And today, I mean it's Valentine's Day. Not exactly the romantic getaway y'all were hoping for, huh?"

He finished taking samples from everything sitting around. We left. I made sure not to touch anything, trying to avoid contamination as much as possible. Maude had done something. Of that, I was certain. I just didn't know what. Or why exactly, though a picture was forming.

Aiden was sitting at a different table watching the EMTs load the young man on a stretcher. The faces had changed. More police were there. Someone was loading up the older couple we'd sat with earlier in a car.

I raised an eyebrow at Aiden.

"Everyone is being taken to the hospital to get blood-work and checked out. If there was some sort of contamination or…" he didn't say the word poison but I knew what he meant.

I nodded at him to keep going.

"They want to check us out. Keep us all for observation," he said. He shuddered. His eyes looked a bit gray around the edges.

"What about Maude?" I asked.

"They've insisted she go, too, but she's been fighting them. Has people coming in later today," Aiden said.

"Some Valentine's Day for us," I said. "And honeymoon. Maybe I should have just taken you on a case. I'm supposed to be on a desk. It'd have been safer."

Aiden smiled. "We can have a redo. Something different."

"Maybe just the Kentucky Castle. Lie in bed in a fancy room. Eat fancy food that I don't understand from their restaurant."

"Or maybe just something in Louisville. Historic..." Aiden trailed off.

"I think this was sort of historic, don't you think?" I asked. "We could go to Asheville."

"Biltmore property would be nice," Aiden agreed.

We smiled at each other. I could have suggested Paris or something and he'd have agreed. Even made it happen. I was sort of the homebody, the one who always wanted things close in case I got called in. I worried about things like that. Aiden could work anywhere. I needed to be around, available.

I said we could drive our own car to the hospital. I got an address from one of the police officers and we took off after I went upstairs and got my things. The rumpled sheets and the room reminded me of how comfortable the place was.

If I were a romantic, I'd be pissed. As it was, except for worrying that something might happen to Aiden, I found this interesting. The puzzle pieces were fascinating to me. Aiden remarked on that on our drive.

"You look a little peaked," I said. "Shadows around your eyes."

"I feel okay," he said. "Maybe a little fatigue. Not sure."

"Do I look okay?" I asked.

"No shadows around your eyes," he said. "And you seem like you feel more energetic than I feel. Of course, you're often more energetic than I am, especially in the morning."

Not once he was up. Aiden might not leap out of bed, but he wasn't one to just lie around. I didn't say anything. I was thinking about breakfast. The Swedish pancake, which everyone ate but me. It could also have been the juice, but I didn't remember others drinking any particular juice. Besides which, Maude had made a big deal out of serving the pancake. I didn't want one, but she sent one out anyway.

We got to the hospital. I let them know that we'd been at Carlton River Castle and were there to be checked out. Aiden was led immediately back. I was called a few moments later. A nurse took blood samples and saliva samples. I was asked to give a urine specimen as well.

I did all of that without any objection. She took my temperature and vitals and sent me out to the waiting area, saying they needed the room. I expected to see Aiden out there, but he wasn't. I waited.

No one came out to tell me anything. I recognized no one in the waiting room as being from the Castle. Something was wrong.

"Excuse me," I said going up to the desk. "My husband is here and I've been waiting. I'm wondering what's going on. They sent me out over an hour ago."

The nurse asked for some information. Then she nodded at the computer, turned away from me so I couldn't see.

"It'll be a bit longer. They're still waiting on test results. I'm sure one of the detectives or a doctor will come speak with you soon," she said.

I stood there, giving her my best glare, hoping the magic of being a detective who understood that silence got people talking would force her to give me some answers, but the admissions nurse was immune to my powers. I eventually walked back across the creamy tile floor to the plastic seats that looked like something I might find in my local DMV.

There were only two other people waiting. I heard plenty of people moving around in the back over the instrumental music they had on the radio. I stood up and began to pace. One by one the other two people in the waiting area were called back. No one came for me. No one told me anything.

I repeated my inquiry at the desk. The nurse was polite but firm. She gave me no information.

More pacing. The clock ticked. I imagined a huge loud tick each time a number changed, though I heard nothing. There were scattered magazines on little plastic tables set in between every fourth chair. From the looks of things, half the town could wait in the waiting room. I paced behind them, looking out as the daylight got brighter and then pinker.

When I could stand it no more I went back to the desk. The nurse gave me the same thing.

"You said that hours ago," I said. "There's no reason to keep me waiting here. I want to see my husband."

"I can't let you do that," she said.

I had watched the doors through which the other two people waiting had gone and I pushed through them myself. The nurse called after me. I heard her on the phone calling for security. If I got removed from the hospital, I'd be calling an attorney and demanding that Aiden be moved to a different hospital. There was no way I was waiting while they did who knows what to my husband.

Beds were filled. I recognized a few people from the B & B. Most were sleeping, some with oxygen on their face. All had IVs. They weren't in actual hospital rooms, just the emergency cubicles. Finally, I reached Aiden's bed.

He, too, had an IV in his arm, though he wasn't on oxygen.

"What's going on?" I asked him, sitting down.

He roused himself.

"They said there was some sort of poison in my system. I've been having some kind of treatment. I asked for you to come back hours ago."

"I've asked about you at the desk multiple times, but the nurse there kept telling me to go sit down and wait. I had enough," I said.

"I'm surprised it took you this long," Aiden laughed.

Security came in.

"You'll have to leave, ma'am," he said.

"This is my husband," I said.

"I want my wife here," Aiden said.

"I have my orders," security said and tried to grab my arm.

Aiden sat up and started fumbling with his IV. They were monitoring him and that set off beeping.

"What's going on?" A nurse demanded as he walked in. His dark hair was bed tousled and he looked frazzled.

"I'm leaving with my wife," Aiden said. "Security says she can't be back here and I'm not staying without her. I'll get records and go to my regular doctor."

The nurse looked at me. "I'm sorry. You can't stay here and the sheriff has ordered that your husband has to. You have to leave."

"This is my husband," I said. "I want to know why I can't be with him, particularly when it's clear he wants to be with me."

"Am I under arrest?" Aiden asked.

"No…" the nurse hesitated.

The security guard was pulling at me. I dragged my feet.

"Then I'm leaving," Aiden said. He started fumbling with the IV.

"That could kill you," the nurse shrieked. "We're only trying to keep you safe."

"I'd feel safer with my wife!" Aiden snapped. "You can't keep me from seeing family. I demand the right to see my wife."

The security guard continued to pull me away. I stepped on his foot, hard. He grunted. The angle meant that it could have been an accident. It bought me some time.

"I can't leave you in the room with a poisoner!" the nurse yelled.

"My wife did not poison me, you jackass," Aiden snapped. "She's an FBI agent. We were on our honeymoon."

"The sheriff says otherwise. She was the only person not infected with the poison," the nurse said.

"What about Maude?" Aiden demanded.

"She had some in her system, too," the nurse said. "Which is why we're looking at your wife."

"Maybe you should look at what I didn't eat that others did," I said. "I have celiac so the pancake that Maude insisted we all have just sat on my plate."

The nurse shook her head.

Security pulled harder, nearly pulling my arm out of the socket. I let him take me even though Aiden was fussing with his IV.

"I'm calling an attorney," I said. "And the office."

I shrugged off the security guard and called my boss first thing. I explained what was going on. He cursed a few times, asked who I had pissed off with my mouth. I said I hadn't had a chance, but would be happy to tell off anyone he wanted me to.

That got a laugh.

Next, I called an attorney. I don't keep a criminal attorney on file, but as law enforcement, I knew many of them. I had someone in mind to call for this. He said he'd send someone up there immediately as this sounded ridiculous, particularly considering I'd never even been advised of my rights.

Then I went back to sit in the waiting room.

The admissions nurse glared at me. She picked up the phone. She didn't tell me to leave.

Security came out. I expected to be escorted out, but he just stood by the doors to the treatment rooms, arms crossed, staring at me. I stared back. I won that particular contest.

By the time that was done, a woman came in, dressed in jeans and a t-shirt. She looked around.

"Jana Baxter?" she asked.

"That's me," I said.

She looked around then nodded. Indicated she was with the law firm I called. I raised an eyebrow impressed that she'd gotten there so fast.

"We have an office only an hour away," she said. "Jack will be here tomorrow but it's late to come out this way tonight and he's hoping I can take care of this. Where's the doctor?"

"I haven't been able to see anyone," I said. "The only reason I even know they suspect me of poisoning people is because the nurse said something when my husband tried to leave with me."

"And they wouldn't let him?" she asked, her voice rising.

I shook my head.

She marched up to the desk and demanded to talk with someone as my attorney.

"I'm sorry but the sheriff has said no one is talk to anyone back there right now while they're investigating."

"Then get the sheriff out here, now."

The nurse shrugged and made a call. Security came over to investigate what was happening.

"I will call the FBI and every single law enforcement agency in the damned state as well as the governor if you put a hand on me," my attorney said. "I have a right to be here and a right to talk to my client's husband who has asked for her though she's not been permitted to see him."

"I was ordered to keep her away from everyone," he said. "Just doing my job."

"You'll let me back?"

"Can't do that. He's not to see anyone. The doctor is afraid he'll pull his IV line out and then she'll kill him." The security guard said all this with a straight face.

Finally, the nurse came back with the sheriff. I hadn't seen him earlier, only the four officers. He didn't look happy about being summoned.

My attorney did her thing. He tried to say no. She pushed the law. When she went back, he tried to prevent me from going with her. She told him he could arrest me now or let me go back to my husband.

He hemmed and hawed, thinking about it.

She reminded him he had nothing on me other than the fact that I was the only one who hadn't gotten sick. And that I had a very good reason for not eating much of the food on the table. Apparently, the sheriff hadn't gotten to the part where I had a disease that would have made eating gluten a problem which meant I'd picked at the eggs and not eaten the pancake at all.

He reluctantly allowed us back to see my husband.

Two other FBI agents arrived at the hospital to find out what was really going on. In short order they discovered that Maude had given herself a low dose of the poison when she'd learned that someone had called the police and hoped to throw suspicion on me. The doctors looking at the amounts of poison suspected that people had been ingesting it for several days. I hadn't been in town for several days and could prove that I was home.

Eventually, I was left alone with my husband, though my attorney stayed around, just in case. Even after Maude was arrested, she stayed around.

"I heard," she said, walking with me, "that she was distraught over her husband leaving her. She hated that the B & B was a romantic place to visit and was poisoning the young couples. Once they caught her in her lies, she admitted that once everyone was down, she was going to lay them out in their beds and light the place on fire. Go out with a bang on Valentine's Day, she said."

I shuddered.

"She hadn't planned on anyone not being interested in the pancake. Unfortunately, she needed something that was likely to have plenty of sweet syrup or jam on it to disguise the flavor of the poison."

I shook my head.

Aiden held my hand. "I read up on my phone that Iceland has very little crime. Like four murders in a year last year. Maybe we ought to go there."

"In summer, maybe?" I suggested.

"I'll see what kind of romantic places they have. I hear it's gorgeous."

"Of course, it's not Valentine's Day," I said. Aiden had really wanted to do something romantic for the holiday.

"I don't know about you, but I'm kind of soured on the day. Maybe I'll feel different next year, but we sure as heck aren't going to go anywhere to eat."

That made me laugh. Knowing Aiden, he would get set on Iceland. It would probably be a far more active vacation than we'd hoped for, but he was right. We weren't likely to run into a murderer no matter where we stayed. And given that I don't speak the language, it was far less likely that I'd piss someone off with my mouth. Not that that had happened here, but better safe than sorry.

BONNIE ELIZABETH WRITES A VARIETY of speculative fiction. In the same way, she's hopped around in a variety of different job fields. She's worked as a veterinary receptionist, cemetery administrator, and as a licensed acupuncturist. Through it all, she wrote stories.

Her novels include gothic novels, contemporary fantasy, paranormal police procedural, paranormal cozy mystery, and paranormal women's fiction. Her short stories have appeared in a number of anthologies and magazines.

She lives in Kentucky with her husband and is bossed around by her three cats. She's currently at work on a cozy fantasy novel.

She is active on Facebook on her page Bonnie Elizabeth and you can reach her through her website, https://BonnieElizabeth.com

Ham a Happy Valentine's Day

By C. A. Rowland

JOSIE STARED AT THE MATERIALS in front of her. She'd signed up for the Ham Radio class with good intentions but hadn't realized the extent of how much math there'd be. Math had never been her strong suit in school. Looking around the conference center's small room, the other men and the other woman taking the class worked away on the examples. She felt like she was back in high school. Lines of rectangular tables with chairs. The instructor with a whiteboard who droned on at times but was engaging at others. Beige walls that made her long for the outdoors and the barn where the elephants were housed. The refuge and the little elephant, Ruan, had kept her sane when Hal died.

She refocused.

She owed this to Hal. He'd been the one who was a member and officer of the group sponsoring these classes for newbies to ham radio or those taking it to learn more about it.

Hal had had the set-up.

That set-up had saved her elephants — and her.

Josie glanced at her watch. She'd be out of here in another hour. She foresaw a long walk in her afternoon to get the kinks out of sitting on a hard chair for four hours.

THE INSTRUCTOR CAME AROUND, AND with his help, Josie finally mastered the questions. Sam was a good man and had known Hal for years. When Hal had taken sick, he'd been one of the first to offer to help her with the farm while Hal recuperated. Hal had declined all offers, and Josie had managed. Until Hal died, and the government came calling about the elephants. It had been a trying time, and in the end, Josie's call for help on the ham radio saved her, the refuge, and the elephants.

She'd determined afterward that becoming a ham radio operator was a necessity.

The 1,000-acre refuge in middle Tennessee was isolated, and it was not uncommon to have unwanted visitors from the nearby hills and forest. Those were mostly the four-legged kind. Since the refuge was open to the public, there had also been a few of the two-legged variety. It was best to be prepared for anything, which was part of her rationale for taking this course. If the phone didn't work, the ham radio most likely would.

Josie stretched and decided she needed a break. She stood up and wandered out the door to grab a breath of fresh air. Winter was here, and the air was cold. She longed for the days when the leaves would start to grow.

Driving to Lawrenceville twice a month for classes had become a treat. It was larger than the town nearest her where she bought her groceries. Now, she timed it so she could browse the antique shops and have a meal before returning to the refuge.

When Hal was alive, they'd driven to various places for an afternoon adventure each month. Not that they wanted to escape since they both loved the animals and being outside, but more that it broke the routine of mucking out stalls and feeding times. Now she found that she had to schedule time away, or she'd simply never leave.

A horn honked, and she jumped. The refuge was off the main roads, so vehicles other than those delivering supplies were fewer. She was more likely to hear an elephant trumpet than a truck horn.

She wondered if the little one, Ruan, had ventured outside the barn. He was still mourning Hal. Josie understood that, and they had bonded as they both grieved.

Josie's two part-time workers also knew to spend time with him so he wasn't lonely. She had to admit she was worried about the little guy, if a three hundred pound anything with feet that could trample you and big ears that could knock you down could be considered small.

Drawing one more deep breath, Josie moved back inside. Another half hour and they'd be done for the day.

Josie opened the door and stepped inside, closing it quietly behind her. As she turned to walk to her table, she noticed an unknown man was talking to the instructor. She didn't recognize him, but clearly, the two knew each other.

"Josie, glad you're back. We're ending early today since we have a visitor," Sam said.

She could feel her face heat up as she smiled and gave a short wave to the instructor. A few steps later, and she sat down.

The man was tall, over six feet, if she had to guess. He was country, at least that was her word for it. Dressed in denim pants with a brown cowboy hat and a pair of boots. His skin was tanned, so he spent a lot of time in the sun. She protected her skin, but Hal's had the same quality. His had been from hard work, if she had to guess.

He was one of a million men or more across the country who used their hands for work, if she had to guess. The kind of man she respected for his work ethic.

"Everyone, I'd like to introduce you to our regional representative, Jack Matters. He's in town on business, and when he learned about the class, he asked to say a few words. I've known him for years, and he's been a good friend to our club. Please welcome him," Sam said.

Josie clapped along with the others in the class. Jack smiled, and she noted it was a genuine smile, not one of those where you felt like the person wanted to be somewhere far, far away.

"Thanks, folks," Jack said. "Ham radio is a passion of mine. It connects us to others we might never be able to talk to. I've had a few late-night conversations with people with differing views, but the discussions have always been lively. It's been my experience that if you're lonely or need help, there's always someone to talk to if you reach out."

Jack paused.

"My being here today is about a different matter. I want to make sure this community remains alive, and with today's technology, it's important we have members trained to operate in the ham radio world from all generations and with all kinds of interests. I'm truly glad to see all of you here learning. I'd like to ask each of you, as you move through the classes and get your licenses, to bring someone else into this community with you. It will make us all stronger. That's all I've got other than I'd love to meet each of you before you leave."

Josie sat back in her chair. She'd been mesmerized by that silky voice. Not that it was smooth. It was rough and rugged, like a man who worked the land. His words had been unexpected, too. They flowed but without any pretense of being practiced or prepared. She wondered if he was a local politician and laughed to herself. He was here from another part of the state. Who he was didn't matter. She'd be nice and then head for home.

The other students rose and headed to the front of the room. Josie gathered her things and walked forward.

As she walked up, Jack looked over the shoulder of the shorter man in front of Josie. She guessed he'd sized her up before she was in front of him, holding out her hand.

"I'm Josie Jenkins," she said with a smile.

Jack took her hand, but before either could say more, Hal said, "Josie was Hal Jenkins' wife."

Josie felt a slight jolt of electricity between them and closed her eyes so Jack wouldn't see any reaction.

Jack's smile faded.

"I'm so sorry. I knew Hal through the club when he came to the regional meetings. He is missed both in our group and I know in your family," Jack said. "He sure could tell a story. I always knew I'd be laughing during any time spent with him."

Josie's legs turned to liquid, and she stared at the ground. She never knew when a word or phrase might stir memories so strong they stopped her cold. This man had known Hal in a different environment, one she hadn't been a part of in a meaningful way, and yet, his words rang true as to Hal's nature.

She took a minute to recover before looking into eyes that held nothing but kindness and sadness. That, more than anything, made her take a step backward. She reached for the table and leaned on it.

Jack was at her side and took her arm, ensuring she didn't fall.

"Are you all right?" Jack asked. "Sam, do you have any water? I think she might need a drink."

Sam headed to the far right of the room and drew out a bottle of water. Josie took a minute and tentatively stood up, still leaning on the table.

"I'm okay. The ham radio club was Hal's interest, and he'd tell me stories from the meetings. What you described was so like him—it caught me by surprise. He's been gone for six months now, but every so often, someone shares a memory that catches me off guard."

Sam returned with the bottle of water and handed it to Josie. She drank deeply and drew in a deep breath. Feeling stronger, she stood without holding onto the table.

"He was a good man. We all loved him, and I understand how you feel. I lost my wife a few years back. I still have those moments, less now, but it can be something small that completely wipes me out," Jack said with a tiny laugh.

"Are you here on ham radio business?" Josie asked, changing the subject. She could hold her own again but wasn't sure whether she could deal with more talk about Hal. And certainly not with someone whose touch had affected her in that way.

JACK SAW THE WOMAN WALK into the conference room as he talked to Sam. She was medium height with long dark hair that cascaded down her back. He could see that flowing behind her as a horse galloped. He almost grinned as he caught himself. He was here to solicit new members for the group, not get a date.

As Sam announced his presence, he got a chance to watch her. She was graceful but with a bit of an awkwardness when she knew people were watching as they were now. Was she just trying out the ham radio, or was she serious? There were many evenings when he dialed in just to talk to someone for a few minutes. Who was she, and why was she here?

He listened to Sam introduce him as he took in the room, always coming back to the woman. When Sam gave him the floor, he realized he hadn't thought about what he'd say. Although he'd spoken to groups many times, he wanted his words to reach these folks.

When it came time to meet the woman, Sam interjected that she was Hal's widow.

Jack almost stumbled over his words as he realized who she was. He'd liked Hal and had heard him speak about Josie. Seeing her in person took him a minute to put what he knew of her from Hal with the woman standing before him.

His memories of Hal seemed to affect her deeply, and she staggered. Her arm was warm, thin, but strong, as if it was made of all muscle. Josie was a woman who worked the refuge as much as Hal had.

As she recovered, she asked him why he was in town.

"I have a business meeting this afternoon with a local banker. We were in college together and try to get together on a regular basis. This class was a good reason to visit," Jack said. "And you own an elephant refuge? I bet there's a story there."

Josie smiled. She could talk about the elephants forever.

"I have four older elephants and one about two years old. We can probably take about two more before we max out. It keeps me busy, but I love it. They are such smart animals."

Jack smiled.

"While I don't have elephants, I have horses on my land. I can't imagine my life without them," he said.

"Um, I hate to cut this short, but the conference closes in five minutes. We need to take this outside," Sam said.

"Thanks. Sam. Appreciate all your help on the math part today. I need to be heading home anyway," Josie said. "And if you're really interested, we're opening the refuge back up next week to the public. Or I open it for friends if they want to visit. Sam has my number and address. It was nice to meet you."

Josie turned and headed to the door. She stepped carefully, still not entirely sure of herself. The long drive home would help clear her head. And if the tears came, she could cry in peace.

Jack watched Josie walk out the door. She still had a slight wobble, but he admired how quickly she had pulled herself together. He'd have been a wreck for a day or so if someone had said his words so quickly after Susan's death. He could kick himself for not realizing who she was. He knew Hal's last name was Jenkins but hadn't connected it in time.

His eyes were drawn to her small waist and confident walk. He'd never understood the attraction of some men to thin women. Josie's body was curvy in all the right places.

"Ready to go?" Sam asked.

"Just admiring the view," Jack said.

Sam laughed. "She's special, all right. You should know that we all thought a lot of Hal. And with that comes looking out for Josie now that he's gone. You get any ideas about her, make sure you're not just messing with her. We wouldn't take kindly to that."

Jack stared at Sam.

"Understood. I've dated only a few women since Susan died, but nothing has been quite right. I don't string them along just because I might be able to. Besides, Josie and I live too far apart for us to see each other much."

The two walked to the door, Sam closed it and then turned to shake hands with Jack.

"Even so, we don't want her hurt. She's endured a lot this past year, and not just Hal's death. But distance can be shortened with ham radio time. Just saying."

Jack laughed.

"I hear you on that. There are more women on the ham radio now than there has been before. But, I take your meaning loud and clear."

WHEN THE PHONE RANG THE next morning, Josie was surprised it was Jack.

"Hey, I know it's short notice, but I have some time before I head back to my home and thought if your offer was still open to visit, I'd swing by," Jack said.

Josie stood, coffee cup in hand, at her sink overlooking the meadow, brown and uninviting. She could nip this in the bud by saying no, but something inside her told her to see where it went. Who knew? She might make a friend she could talk to on the ham radio.

The shed Hal had assembled stood on one side of the meadow — in the trees so it was mostly hidden — but near the ham radio tower with a clear line of sight for transmissions. All his equipment was there, including the small, hidden underground safe for essential papers and his licenses. She hadn't ventured out there in months. Maybe it was time to do that. She could show Jack the set-up and ask his opinion on any changes she might need to make.

Or not. Would that be too weird? For one or both of them?

In any event, Jack was waiting for an answer.

"Sure, come on by. The elephants are in the barn due to the cold. We've got a bit of heating, but make sure you wear your coat. I've got hot chocolate or something stronger to help with the cold, too. Do you have the address?" Josie asked.

"That all sounds good. Sam gave me the address, and I'll use the GPS. I'll be there in an hour or so. Anything else I need to know?"

"The roads have a few sharp curves. I'd watch your speed limit. And Smithers has a deputy sheriff who loves to give out tickets to strangers. It's a speed trap for sure."

"Good to know," Jack said. "I'll see you soon."

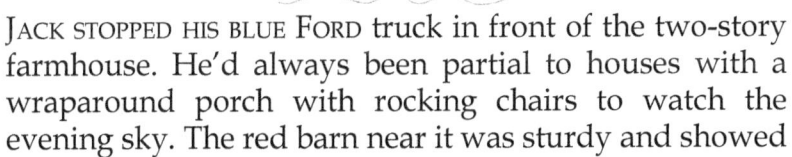

JACK STOPPED HIS BLUE FORD truck in front of the two-story farmhouse. He'd always been partial to houses with a wraparound porch with rocking chairs to watch the evening sky. The red barn near it was sturdy and showed some wear in patches, but mostly, he liked what he saw. The land and buildings were cared for. He suspected the animals were too.

As a figure came out of the barn, he smiled. Josie was in jeans and a plaid shirt, her hair pulled back into a ponytail. She lifted her arm to swipe away sweat despite the temperature being in the 30s. He liked a woman who could work and play hard, but running this operation had to be taking its toll on her.

Josie waved.

Jack walked forward.

"Did you have any trouble finding us?" she asked.

"No, but I was glad for the warning on speeding. Your deputy was hidden well. I waved to him as I went by. Not sure that set too well with him," Jack said.

Josie laughed.

"Nope, he likes the speeders. But, it's chilly out here. Come into the barn. I'll show you around, and then we can have a cup of coffee or something."

Jack nodded as she turned.

He followed her inside to what turned out to be a fairly typical setup of stalls on each side with a wide section down the middle for moving the animals in and out. The difference was in scale. Each stall in the front held one elephant, so it was three times the size of a regular stall holding his horses. The stalls at the back were smaller, at only twice the size. There was what could only be called a shower in one back corner where Josie must wash the elephants and a closed room in the other corner.

Jack jumped when the first elephant trumpeted. He'd told himself he'd hear that on the way over. Still, being there when it sounded and seemed to echo through the barn, he couldn't control his reaction.

The second and third trumpets were loud but didn't affect him as much. However, the whole sound and realization that live elephants were twice his size was unnerving. How on Earth did Josie deal with these?

He had almost calmed down when the littlest elephant—Josie had called him Ruan—trumpeted and ran toward him. Jack stumbled back a couple of steps before realizing he needed to stand his ground.

Ruan ran up to him and stopped just short. The little elephant kept trumpeting. and Josie walked over to see if she could calm him.

"Shush," she said.

Ruan continued, and Jack said between blasts, "Why don't we go outside?"

Josie nodded and began to shepherd the elephant back to his stall. Jack turned and walked outside.

Jack stood for a minute until Josie joined him.

"He seems protective of you," Jack said.

"Ruan is also mourning. I've learned a lot more about elephants since Hal died. He and Ruan had bonded. Hal's death sent him into a spiral. Now, he tends to shadow me or the workers he knows when we are around."

Josie paused.

"So, what do you think? The barn houses the elephants, and we have some areas for them to graze when the grass is growing. Over there, you can see the ham radio tower. The shed by it is where the set-up is. Would you like to see it?" Josie asked.

Jack hesitated. That would be Hal's domain. He wasn't sure what his being there would trigger for Josie.

"Don't worry, I have been in there alone. Besides, I'd like your professional opinion as a ham operator regional representative on what's there," she said.

Jack laughed.

"That is some kind of pretentious title you've laid on me. I hope I can live up to it. Let's go," he said.

They walked toward the shed.

"This place must be beautiful in the spring when all the trees have leaves," Jack said.

"It is. But I love the winter as well. The lack of leaves lets me see behind the foliage to what's mostly hidden unless I hike around in the forest. It's totally different, and that's fun too."

Jack hadn't considered that since his winter outdoor rides were mainly to help find missing animals or keep the other animals fed and warm.

At the shed's door, Josie drew out keys and unlocked it.

Jack arched an eyebrow. This place was pretty isolated, but he was used to sheds being unlocked.

Inside, Jack understood. He whistled in appreciation. Hal had quite the setup.

"Wow, this is great. Hal had top-of-the-line equipment from his transceiver to his power source," Jack said.

JOSIE STOOD BACK AS JACK moved closer and examined how Hal had set up his system. She'd known he had quality equipment. If there was one thing he insisted on, it was quality tools.

Jack sat down at the table holding the ham radio. Josie watched him inspect each piece before moving on. He was methodical in a way Hal wasn't.

She let a breath out that she hadn't realized she'd been holding. Jack being here was okay.

"Some of this is more advanced than a beginner setup would have. Is Sam or someone available to walk you through this if you have questions?" Jack asked.

"Are you offering your expertise?" Josie asked.

She felt her face warm as she said that. Josie hadn't flirted with a man, other than Hal, in years. What was she thinking? This man lived hours away from her. They both had farms that required daily attention. Still, it was fun when he turned to her, a look of surprise on his face that turned mischievous.

"I might be if the right person is asking," Jack said.

Josie grinned as Jack rubbed his hands together and blew on them.

"Seen enough, or would you like to stay here longer? There's a cup of coffee with your name on it in my kitchen whenever you're ready."

Jack smiled.

"Coffee sounds good, and as much as I'd like to hang out and see what else is part of this system, I have somewhere to be before I head home.

AND THERE IT WAS. RIGHT in his face. He had a home miles away with responsibilities at least as great as Josie's. What was he doing? Their two worlds were similar but too far apart to work. Neither could be gone from their land for long. If Josie was who he thought she was, she would be as uncomfortable with delegating her responsibilities as he would be.

He followed her across the meadow, the porch, and into a warm kitchen. He sat at the wooden table, which showed marks of use and love over the years. Jack could almost hear the sounds of fights and laughter of those who had sat here before him. It was almost as if the house was welcoming him in a way that Ruan and the barn had not.

Jack drank the coffee Josie placed in front of him.

They were both quiet as the chill in their hands and body seemed to cool the air in the kitchen.

Jack wondered if coming here had been a mistake. He decided to address the elephant in the room, so to speak.

"Look, I don't like to play games, so I'm just going to say this out loud. I like you. I'd like to get to know you better. We live far apart, so seeing you often is not an option. How about we agree to talk on the ham radio and get to know each other better that way?"

Josie considered his offer. It was a good one, and she was pragmatic about the situation.

"I'd love to do that. I have a hard time getting away for the classes, let alone time for dinner or travel right now. But a friend I could use if you are okay with that."

Jack nodded.

He drank the last of his coffee and got up.

"Then we are agreed. I thank you for the tour. I'll let you say goodbye to Ruan and the other elephants. Let's stay in touch. If you're out my way, let me know. I'd love to show you my farm and treat you to a meal. I'll do the same when I am here," Jack said as he headed to the door.

Josie followed him.

Jack got in his truck and headed out.

A part of her felt like she had just lost something. But she couldn't figure out how to keep it or how there might be a different future for her and Jack.

Jack read the email from Sam about the celebration party of the ham radio group. They had three new members who had recently received their licenses. Josie was one of them.

Jack could easily rearrange his schedule to include meetings plus attend the party. The only problem was it was also Valentine's Day. Sam had said there would be lots of singles attending since a number of the members were widowers or widows or divorced.

What message would he be sending Josie if he attended? They had started talking over the ham radio, but he hadn't been back in town.

He closed the email, not sure what he would do.

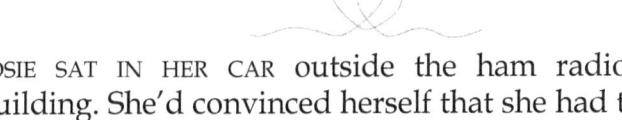

JOSIE SAT IN HER CAR outside the ham radio meeting building. She'd convinced herself that she had to come to the party since, at least in part, it was for her and her new license. That didn't bother her. It being on February 14th and Valentine's Day was the issue.

Her hands were shaking at the thought of being alone at a party full of couples. Sam had assured her she wouldn't be the only single there, but she was going home if she couldn't get her hands to stop shaking.

Sitting there, she watched a familiar blue truck pull into the parking lot.

Jack was here.

Now, she really didn't know what to do. Her hands had calmed down, but her heart was racing at the thought of seeing him again. They'd had a few long conversations on the ham radio, and from what she'd learned she liked him even more now. Was it a coincidence that he was in town, maybe for meetings? Or had he come to see her or celebrate with her?

Josie hadn't backed down from many challenges and she figured now was not the time to start. She opened her door, straightened her dress, and headed inside.

JACK WAS LOOKING AROUND THE beige room that seemed to be marked by red hearts on the tables and walls when he felt a breeze from the front door opening. His eyes widened at Josie. He'd liked how she fit into her jeans, but the black dress took his breath away. Whatever was he thinking when he decided to come to this party? It had been a hair-brained idea that had seemed like a good one at the time.

He was here, so he might as well go with it. Nothing like going all in. He moved between the partygoers, always keeping Josie in sight. Driving over, he'd had a thought. A weird, crazy idea of how they might continue to grow their relationship from being friends to something more.

In the light of the room, he wasn't sure he could even say the words. She was going to think he was nuts. He even thought that right now.

Jack reached the table with hors d'oeuvres.

Josie stepped up at the same time.

"Fancy meeting you here," she said.

He laughed, thankful she had a silly opening line since he'd lost his ability to talk.

"I had a meeting, and frankly, I wanted to see you and say congratulations on your license," Jack said.

"Copy that," Josie said, trying on the slang for the word understand in ham radio speak. "I'm glad you're here."

Jack smiled. He knew what it was like trying to get comfortable with all the codes and shorthand that ham radio operators used. Josie would be fine with all of this once she had a bit more time on the radio.

"I wasn't sure I should come," Jack said. "I know we agreed to be friends."

Josie nodded.

"I had a thought that may sound totally ridiculous. So, hear me out on this before you dismiss it or start laughing."

Josie waited.

"You have the refuge, and I have the farm. We both have animals that need care, as well as the buildings and everything else. Our employees can take care of those for short periods. But we're both responsible adults and don't want to leave the care of animals to others for too long."

He paused.

"Okay. So, I've been reading about elephants. They migrate each year. It's built into their makeup so that they can remember where to go each year. And it's passed down. So, I got to thinking, do your elephants miss that? What if they had a new migration pattern? Would that add to their knowledge? Would it make them happy?"

Josie had to turn her head to keep from laughing. She had a full visual of a picture her aunt had given her from a small Wyoming town. In it were single-story buildings and current model cars. The main drag had a cattle herd being handled by a few cowboys on horses. The title had been "Rush Hour Traffic."

"Sorry, it's a silly idea. I shouldn't have even brought it up," Jack said.

"No," Josie said as she touched his arm. She described the picture and continued, "But instead of cattle, I had this picture of elephants headed down the streets. I didn't mean to hurt your feelings. It was just so vivid in my head."

He stared at her while thinking of where to begin again.

"It's a creative idea. Or at least it's an alternative to what we've been doing. I've racked my brain for ideas of how we could spend more time together but not neglect our animals. From your description, your place is large enough to house the elephants if we brought them there. And mine can accommodate more horses. The question is, how would we move them, and would that have any negative effects? We both have houses big enough for guests, so staying over shouldn't be an issue. There are other details about the refuge, and it being open to the public. I'm not sure, but it's a start on thinking about how we might do this," Josie said.

Jack sighed, and the knot in his shoulders relaxed some. He hadn't realized how tense he was. Moving was what he needed.

"I'd like to explore that and any other options. I like you, and while I've enjoyed talking to you, I'd like to spend more time in person—if we can figure out how," Jack said.

"Good plan," Josie said. She liked the fact that he was open to compromise.

A country western tune started on the audio equipment in one corner. Jack looked at Josie.

"Care to dance while we figure this out?" he asked.

Josie smiled as she moved to the dance floor, where Jack took her in his arms. He planned to keep her there during the party.

As they moved across the floor, he asked, "There's a little place I know that has great food. Will you have dinner with me?"

Josie's eyes shone as she nodded. She wasn't sure how this would work out, but she knew they could find a way if they worked together. For now, she wanted to enjoy being in his arms and his presence. He guided her into a turn, and they two-stepped across the dance floor.

C.A. ROWLAND IS A recovering lawyer turned writer. Raised in Texas, she now calls Tennessee home – a place of history, folklore and inspiration. She's published short stories and is currently finishing the second in her amateur sleuth mystery set in Savannah, Georgia.

For more information, see https://carowland.com.

Cosima's Heart's Desire

By Johanna Rothman

COSIMA WATERHOUSE LOVED HER JOB at the LocalPharm—yes, the local pharmacy in her little Arlington neighborhood, just west of Cambridge and all those universities in the great state of Massachusetts. Except for today, Valentine's Day.

Personally, Cosima didn't see the point of Valentine's Day. All that hoopla over one day, to find your heart's desire? She knew that the point of a happily ever after was about maintaining a relationship over time. And she just did not have the time or the interest—not if she was going to graduate in two years. She wouldn't mind setting this store to rights or to make more money. But a heart's desire? Nah. She'd leave that for the romantics. In the meantime, she could bask in their happiness.

At high noon, She had no basking because the store was full of people shopping for their candy and cards—never mind their prescriptions or other necessities.

She could tell from the crinkling of the candy bags and the people ooh-ing and aah-ing over cards—all excellent noises today. She'd already restocked both the candy and card aisles twice. She wasn't sure they'd make it until closing at nine without running out of candy and cards.

A good problem to have.

She was running around because her boss, whom she'd nicknamed miser-Mark—aka Mark Mason—had filled the store with icky odors of metallic green beans and stale roses. Most of the customers were in such a rush to

JOHANNA ROTHMAN

shop and leave that Cosima helped them find what they wanted.

Cosima called him miser-Mark because he always took the cheap path. It didn't matter if it was the odors or the music—or, today, both.

For some unknown reason, Mark had decided that no one should smell the sweet odor of candy as Cosima would have chosen. No. He'd decided to fill the store with the metallic odor of cooked canned green beans that reminded Cosima of her childhood, and not in a good way. That would have been bad enough, but somehow, he'd added stale roses to the mix.

Ugh. Cosima liked both canned green beans—as long as they were reasonably recent—and fresh roses. But these odors together? It was a Great Big Wrongness.

Worse, that odor had triggered her coughing and sneezing. The rose odor got stuck in her nose, so she sneezed. Then, when she smelled the metal of the canned green beans, she coughed. To fix both, she'd dragged her water bottle all over the store today. That's when she discovered the cap didn't quite fit. She'd dribbled a little water every so often on the dark gray indoor/outdoor carpet that miser-Mark had installed throughout the store. Even the two-foot-wide diameter shiny bright red hearts strategically placed every six feet on that terrible floor could not brighten up the place.

If she owned this place, she'd upgrade everything—the floor, the ceiling, the shelves—everything so that people would want to shop for longer. But miser-Mark never asked her what she thought.

Then, there was the somnambulant music. If any of the rock and roll legends—including the Boss himself, Bruce Springsteen—knew what this subscription service had done to their music, well, murder would be on the menu. The only reason they had that music was because miser-Mark was too cheap to pay for the next-level of subscription. That level encouraged people to tap their feet and shake their booties. Cosima grinned—now that would be a Valentine's Day to remember.

This subscription put everyone to sleep, including two senior citizens waiting for their prescriptions. They only had thirty-minute wait times, but the music had done its magic.

Even she had gotten into the Valentine's Day mood with her warm red turtleneck underneath her matching v-neck red sweater. She'd decorated that sweater with glittery white hearts and snowflakes in honor of the wintry day. She still wore her black jeans, with her blue and green sneakers, because she knew she'd be stocking and unstocking today. But she was as festive as she could be. As miser-Mark had demanded.

She looked around the card aisle in the middle of the store, the pretty bright red and pastel pink cards, what she called the lovey-dovey cards snuggled in their specific slots. The humorous cards next to them, in a rainbow of colors. And finally, the Goth cards, mostly in black.

Cosima didn't understand the black cards, but she figured even Goth people could use a little happiness on Valentine's Day.

She heard the rustling on the other side of the aisle where the candy was. Then she heard an older querulous female voice ask, "Miss? Miss?"

She grinned. Time to restock the candy.

She turned and came face to face with a half-naked baby-like being with a big mop of dark brown hair and big blue eyes standing on the floor directly in front of her. He was significantly shorter than she was—maybe three feet tall, compared to her five-four. His big smile and big round cheeks made her want to smile back at him. Until she saw the falling-down diaper, his hands clutching a brown bow, and a quiver of pale gold arrows on his back.

She had no idea what kind of a baby would wear a diaper and arrows, and carry a bow. In Boston. On a cold February day. Nothing made sense. "Uh, are you missing your mother?" she asked.

His low gravelly voice replied, "My mother? Don't think so, darlin'. I'm on my own now, and have been for centuries. Just looking for my next vic—er, subject. I give people their heart's desires." He paused. "Where are the cigarettes? I need a drag."

Cosima shook her head. "We don't sell cigarettes. Not anymore." Then she took another long look at him. "You're Cupid!" she said.

"Give the woman a prize." He looked around and notched an arrow in his bow.

"Please don't shoot anyone," she said. "No one needs that."

"How do you know what they need? Everyone needs to find their heart's desire."

She sneezed again—the odors were really slowing her down if she'd missed identifying Cupid. She chugged a few sips from her water bottle. Then she said, "I don't care what you do elsewhere, but please don't give people their 'heart's desire' in here. They come for cards and candy, not their heart's desire."

"How do you know what they come in here for?" he asked. "Why wouldn't they come here for their heart's desire? Since you're so close-minded, I'll just go visit the candy aisle."

He flew up and over the aisle separators, hovering just below the ceiling.

"Hey!" Cosima whisper-yelled, trying to get his attention. "Come down from there! Now!"

He offered her an evil grin, and said, "Make me."

She said in a low voice, "Don't make me ask twice." Although, she had no idea what she was going to do.

"Ooh, that sounds exactly like something I want to do

then," he said, his voice sounding rougher than before. "Make me." He grinned again, and dropped down into the candy aisle, below Cosima's sight.

That's when she remembered the voice that sounded like an older woman. She was in that aisle.

Cosima rounded the corner and skidded to a stop. Cupid was now hovering over the woman, just below the aisle separators. He was still a good three feet above her short, curly, salon-colored blue-white hair. He was busy shooting arrows at her tush. But her long, light blue, down coat was not just impermeable to Boston winters, but all the arrows, too. There was a pile of bounced-off arrows behind her on the floor.

He swore quietly.

Rushing around the older woman, Cosima bent down to pick the arrows up off the floor. As she did, she glared at Cupid, who gave her a dirty grin. Maybe the older woman hadn't heard the cursing.

As Cosima stood, she examined the arrows. They were surprisingly light for arrows—almost feeling like they were balsa wood. There was no way these arrows would penetrate anything. Not even summer slacks.

Worse, the arrows felt greasy on her fingers. She looked down at her hands.

The golden color came off on her fingers. These arrows were not robust in any way. Was this guy really Cupid? She didn't know and didn't care. She'd put these behind the registers and then return to the card aisle to see what needed restocking.

That's when she heard the woman again say in that shaky voice, "Miss? Miss?"

She turned and stuck the arrows behind her back. Then she smiled at the older, petite woman who returned that smile with a beaming grin of her own.

The older woman said, "I'm looking for a special card, if you know what I mean." She then winked at Cosima.

Cosima smiled and said, "We have all kinds of cards. Would you like something about being in love?"

The petite older woman laughed and said, "No! Not at all! I want a card about getting it on!"

Cosima's mouth dropped open. She shut it almost as fast—mostly because of the metallic green beans odor.

In response, the older woman grinned. Then she said, "We get it on the same way you young folks get it on. But this time, I'm thinking of a much younger man. Do you have any cougar cards?"

"Cougar cards?" Cosima asked. "The kind about animals??" None of this made sense to her.

"No, dear," the older woman said. "The kind with older women and younger men. I still have some spring in my step and February is way too cold to spend alone. I need a man to warm me up." She smiled. "Oh, you can call me Rose, since I suspect we'll spend a little time together today." Then she winked at Cosima.

Cosima wondered what universe she was living in to discuss getting anything on with an obviously very senior citizen, this Rose. This was the last conversation she expected—or wanted—to have today. She hadn't expected a conversation with Cupid, either.

That's when the diaper-wearing cherub swished down, with a flourish. "Madam," he said, his voice growling as ever, "I have magic arrows. You won't need a card. Instead, point out the person you want to get it on with, and I'll help you along. I can give you your heart's desire."

"Aren't you a dearie," she said. "But I don't want my heart involved. This is just physical."

Cosima's mouth had dropped open again. This woman was talking to Cupid as if he was normal?

"I got ya, either way," he said.

"But I'm really *not* in the market for love," she said, as her blue-white curls bounced a little. "I was lucky once. I won't get that kind of lucky again. I want the other kind of lucky!"

Cupid shrugged. "I'm not picky. You choose someone. I'll nail 'im with an arrow. Then you can get lucky and maybe find another love."

The older woman shook her head, and said, "No, thank you kindly. I don't want a man—or a woman—for *love* on Valentine's Day. I'm in the mood to get it on with someone without any strings attached."

Cupid cocked his head to one side and looked the woman up and down. Then he smiled. "You can have me. Right here. Right now." He started to rub his crotch through the diaper.

Disgusted, Cosima grabbed at his arm to try to pull him away. "Stop that!" she said. "Normal people don't proposition people in the pharmacy. They don't offer a 'right here, right now'. And they certainly don't start getting ready." She shook her head. "This is just ridiculous. You need to leave—now!"

Rose said, "Hold on a second, dearie." She cocked her head sideways to assess Cupid up and down. Cupid did the same, right back at her.

Cosima could not believe what she was seeing.

Then, Rose said, "No. He's too short. Even for me. I want a taller man."

Cupid started to pull down his diaper, "I got the goods—"

"Absolutely not," Cosima said. "I don't care what you have. Pull that diaper up because I do not want to see any more of you than what I already see. I don't care that it's crazy cold outside. You're leaving now. I'm throwing you out."

She clamped onto his left arm with her right and

dragged him to the front of the card aisle. She could see the automatic front doors, just thirty feet away, past several Valentine's Day displays of candy and one display of winter skin moisturizer.

He sputtered a little as they started to walk past one candy display. Then he said, "Don't kick me out. If you keep walking me out, I'll wreck the displays."

Cosima didn't say a word as she continued to drag him to the front door.

But he dragged his feet on the carpet.

Cosima pulled harder on his arm. And then, several things seemed to happen all at once. She slipped on one of the shiny red hearts, right near a candy display. As she fell, she released his arm.

Cupid flew to the top of the display and pushed all the bags of candy over onto her. The many red, brown, and gold bags of candy landed on her, almost pinning her to the floor. She didn't want to wreck the candy, so she carefully rolled to a sitting position, moving bags of candy just as carefully as she proceeded.

By the time she sat up all the way, Cupid was high up at the ceiling. He gave her an evil grin, turned around, pulled down his diaper and mooned her.

She shook her fist at him and thought that this was the most ridiculous Valentine's Day ever.

AFTER RESTORING THE CANDY DISPLAY, Cosima looked up at the ceiling. That ridiculous cherub was gone, at least from directly above her. However, miser-Mike stood right next to her. He wore a red sweater that said, "I'll be your Valentine" over a light blue button-down shirt and charcoal gray slacks. "Hurry up," he said. "While you've been rolling around on the floor, the cards are almost empty. It's time for you to restock."

Based on his personality, Cosima wondered how anyone could find him attractive. She tamped down her irritation and said, "Now that I'm done here, I'm happy to. Did you see Cupid anywhere?"

"Cupid? Are you nuts?"

"You didn't see a very short guy with a curly mop of dark hair? Diaper? Brown bow and gold arrows? The short guy I was trying to escort out before he destroyed this display and I landed on the floor. Him."

Miser-Mark said, "If you're doing drugs and hallucinating, I'm going to need to fire you."

She shook her head. "I'm not doing anything except working. You didn't see him?"

"Of course not. There was no 'Cupid' here. None at all." He shook his head. "If you can't control your hallucinations, you won't have a job here."

Cosima bit back any words she'd considered—and she'd considered plenty. "I'll get to those cards now."

"See that you do."

That was miser-Mark—always blaming her for something. She'd have to think about whether this job was still worth it. Maybe she could find another way to pay for school. In the meantime, she'd restock the cards. And make sure that Cupid was gone.

ABOUT TEN MINUTES LATER, COSIMA returned with a rolling gray cart with plenty of cards. Since there were so many people in the aisle, she decided to push the cart— carefully into the aisle. "Excuse me," she said quietly, "Excuse me."

People maneuvered in and out of her way. But some stopped when she did, and started to look at the cards on her cart. She decided to leave the cart in the aisle and restock from where she was.

"Ladies and gentlemen," she said in a slightly raised voice. "I'm restocking the cards. If you prefer, you can take them from the cart. The lovey-dovey cards are here," as she pointed left, "the humorous cards are in the middle." Then she pointed right and said, "The Goth cards are here."

The people mobbed the cart.

"One more thing," she said. "I have plenty more cards in the back. Plenty. You don't need to fight over a card. I can get you more. I'll restock as you look through the cards, and we'll all be happy."

Cosima started to refill the lovey-dovey cards while she heard people exclaiming, "Oh, look at that!" She turned around to see Cupid hovering over the crowd, trying to notch an arrow in his bow.

"Please come down from there," she said. "I really don't want you to hurt anyone."

Cupid yelled in that growly voice, "Who wants their heart's desire?"

That's when a man, in a black down jacket and black jeans, halfway down the aisle, said, "I do! Hit me, Cupid, hit me!" he lifted his face to Cupid.

"No!" Cosima yelled. "Not his face! Never a face! Those are arrows."

"Very well," the man said. "Here's my neck. Pretend like your arrow is a vampire and you'll go for my neck."

"NO!! Not the neck either! Too many blood vessels. Not the neck!"

That's when the man turned around to Cupid, picked up his jacket and said, "Go for it, Cupid!"

As she pushed through the crowd, Cosima really hoped he'd left his jeans up. Cupid let his arrow fly and hit the man's jeans, just as she got there.

Just a second or two too late.

The arrow fell on the floor, so she picked it up.

"What?" the man in the black jacket asked. "Goth people don't get their happily ever afters? We don't get our heart's desires?"

Cosima started to say, "No—"

That's when Rose rushed up. "I'm going to call the manager," she said. "Everyone here wants their heart's desire. Why should you get all the arrows and us not get any?"

Cosima stood there with her mouth open. Then the green bean odor hit her again, so she snapped it shut.

Cupid asked, "Yeah, why?"

More people milled about her, asking "Why?"

One of the women pushed her.

That was it. Then she had an idea. "Okay, here's what we'll do. Anyone who wants that guy," as she pointed to Cupid, "to shoot them with an arrow, you line up over there." She pointed to the end of the aisle, a narrow aisle that led to the pharmacy area. "Line up nicely, one person in front of the other. I'll get Cupid to shoot you in the leg—"

Cupid glared at her and said, "Tush. Always the tush."

"Fine," she said. "The tush. Carefully, right?"

"Careful is my middle name," he said with that growl again.

She shook her head a little. That she doubted. "Once you get him to shoot you with his arrow, please do continue your shopping. By then, I bet I'll have the cards all restocked."

"The candy, too?" asked a male voice from the crowd.

"Of course," she said. "Candy, too."

Immediately, the aisle emptied as everyone lined up for Cupid to shoot them.

This was the most ridiculous Valentine's Day she'd ever seen. At all.

But all she had to do was restock the cards—and the candy—and then, maybe things would get back to normal.

Less than two minutes later, she heard the first rumblings of trouble. "Miss? Miss?"

Cosima decided that voice sounded like Rose. She rushed over to the line of people waiting for Cupid to shoot them. Rose was at the front. Cupid was shaking his head at her.

"Miss? Cupid won't shoot me," Rose said.

All Cosima could think was that she had not expected anything like this when she'd gotten up this morning. What were people thinking??

"Uh, Cupid, why won't you shoot Rose?"

"Because she's too old."

"You're old, too," Cosima said. "You said you were doing this for centuries. Rose is in line. You should shoot her." Cosima frowned. "That came out wrong, but you should shoot her so she gets her heart's desire."

"She doesn't want a heart's desire," Cupid said, in that gravelly voice.

"Yes, I do!" Rose said.

Several people behind her in line said, "Yes! Yes!"

"She just wants to get laid," Cupid said.

"I do, too! That's my heart's desire," yelled a male voice.

"You're a man—that's all men ever want," said a female voice.

"That's right!" the male voice agreed.

Luckily, the people in line laughed, but Cosima realized she had no control over any of this. Her stomach started to churn.

That's when miser-Mark strolled over. "What's going on here?" He put his hands on his hips, as if he was ready for a fight.

Rose said, "I want Cupid to shoot me so I can get my heart's desire."

"Cupid? That idea again? Where the heck is this Cupid, anyway?"

Cosima looked at Mark and pointed up above his head where Cupid was hovering. "Right up there."

Several other voices said, "Right there," and they pointed to the ceiling.

Mark looked up. "Hey! Get down from there. I don't want you to mess up my ceiling. That ceiling cost me good money!"

That's when Cupid nudged one of the ceiling tiles. A little shower of dust and Styrofoam bits fell when Cupid nudged the tile. Cupid looked down and said, "That's the cheapest kind of ceiling tile there is. What kind of money could it have possibly cost you?"

Mark stood there with his mouth open.

That's when Cupid started to push and pull at another ceiling tile.

Mark turned to Cosima and said, "Stop him! He's going to wreck the store!"

She said, "You're taller than I am. You grab his legs, and this time, when I try to eject him from the store, let me do that!"

"If I have to do this alone, you're fired!"

Cosima rolled her eyes. She'd had it. "Stop with the threatening to fire me business! Now, you get his legs and start to pull."

Mark jumped up, but Cupid flew just far enough away that Mark missed. Mark followed him, but Cupid continued to fly away, making Mark look like he was playing basketball, not someone managing a pharmacy.

As Cupid floated to and fro, he asked, "What will you give me to stop?"

Mark was breathing too heavily to answer.

Cosima asked, "What do you want?"

Cupid looked directly at Mark and said, "I want to give him his heart's desire. Just him."

Cosima heard some "Aw, no" and "I still want my heart's desire" shouts. But the rest of the crowd got very quiet. Then, one guy said, "Do it, man. You own this place? You need your heart's desire. Cupid, do it!"

That's when the crowd changed, "Do it! Do it! Do it!"

"Fine," Mark said. "Those arrows look fake anyway. What do I have to lose?"

He turned to Cupid and said, "Okay, shoot."

"In the tush," Cupid said.

"Okay, okay," Mark said and turned around.

"Bend over a little," Cupid said.

Mark rolled his eyes.

Cosima held her breath.

Cupid drew an arrow from his quiver. This one looked a little different, as if it was real gold. Then, Cupid shot Mark in the tush.

Mark yelped and said, "That hurt!"

Then he paused and said, "I don't feel any different."

Cosima thought he looked the same, too.

That's when Rose walked by and said, "If none of *us* gets our heart's desires, I'm going back to look for a card. And some chocolate, just for me."

Mark followed her with his eyes. Then he jogged after her, saying, "Madam! Madam!"

Cosima turned to Cupid and asked, "What did you do?"

Cupid took out a cigar from his diaper and stuck it in his mouth. "I gave him his heart's desire. What did you think I did?"

Cosima shook her head.

That's when the crowd surged forward, practically trampling her. She heard, "I want my heart's desire, too!"

"Me too!"

"Don't leave me out!"

IN THE LESS THAN TWO minutes it took for Cosima to regain her balance, the crowd had turned into a mob. Everyone was pushing and shoving and yelling. But now, the crowd was yelling for Cupid.

"Cupid! Cupid! Cupid!"

Cosima put her fingers to her lips and created an ear-piercing whistle. She could feel the blood rush to her face, but she didn't care. She was going to create order out of this chaos or her name wasn't Cosima. And it was.

Everyone stopped talking to look around and see who had made that noise.

She took a deep breath in and settled her stomach. Then she yelled, "Everyone! Now that I have your attention, we will be orderly and calm. Cupid, get that diapered tush over here. NOW!"

Cupid flew over, a broad smile on his face. "Yes, ma'am! What can I do for you?"

"You give each and every one of these nice people their damn heart's desires. Now! Arrows or not. You give them what they want. NOW!"

"Uh," he said. "About that—"

"No excuses! You give them what they want. Well, as long as it's legal."

She started to cool off now that she was creating order.

"Uh, I don't think I can."

"WHAT DO YOU MEAN?" she asked. "You riled these nice people up. They thought they would get their heart's desires. Now you can't fulfill that promise? What kind of a Cupid are you?"

"Not a very good one, sorry."

He floated down to the floor and stood directly on a red foil heart. He looked sad, almost as if he was about to cry.

Cosima crossed her arms. She'd seen acts like this before. No way was she going to fall for it again. People—

especially the male kind of people—had done this before. It was always, "It's me, not you." It damn well was them.

"What are you going to do about it?" she asked. "You promised them their heart's desire. Now what?"

"I'll just leave," he said.

"No!" she said. "Don't even think about leaving until you tell me what's going on."

"Yeah," someone said.

"I want to know, too," another voice said.

More and more of the crowd said, "Me too!"

"Start talking," Cosima said. "And make it good."

Cupid said, "Once upon a time—"

Cosima interrupted him. "Don't bother with the origin story. Get to the good parts."

"Yeah," a male voice said, "The good parts!"

Some people in the crowd laughed.

"I screwed up and got a married man with one of my arrows. But I didn't realize he was married or that he was married to a witch."

"It's always the woman's fault!" a female voice yelled. "Now you're going to tell us she cursed you."

"Actually," Cupid said, "No. He cursed me because he was afraid of her."

A woman in the crowd yelled, "Serves you right."

Cosima agreed and heard a few more yeahs from the crowd.

"So I only get one good arrow every year for the next four years. I have to find a big enough crowd that I can find and fulfill a real heart's desire. Otherwise, I'll lose my bow and arrows forever."

"Oh, that's why your previous arrows were too lightweight and the gold rubbed off."

"Yeah," Cupid said. "But I found someone who was perfect."

That's when miser-Mark came jogging around the

corner. "Rose! Rose! Let's go somewhere special." He waggled his eyebrows.

Cosima thought she just might vomit. The only thing worse than blaming-Mark or miser-Mark was this strange get-it-on-Mark.

Rose emerged from the crowd and stood there, looking Mark up and down. "I'll go with you on one condition," she said.

"Name it!"

"Give Cosima the store, so she can do the job you're not doing here. Free and clear. No debts. No nothing. She can make it work."

Cosima raised her eyebrows. Was Mark willing to do this?

He dug in his pocket and pulled out his work keyring. "Done!" he said and tossed them to Cosima. "I'll do paperwork with you later."

She caught them and held on tight.

Mark swung Rose up into his arms and ran out of the store.

Everyone applauded.

By nine that night, Cosima was more than ready to close the store. Mark had signed over LocalPharm to her in total. She really hoped Mark and Rose were having a good time together.

She'd discovered the odors were from two expired odor-plugins. She'd promptly unplugged them, threw them in the trash, knotted the bag and taken it outside to the large green trash bin.

She'd also stopped the terrible music and was all set to look into a better quality music service.

She'd hired a couple of other college—and high school—students to help her run the store and she had a workable schedule, at least for the rest of February.

And Cupid had finally left. He'd managed to discover one more good arrow. He'd hit a Goth man with it. That man had found a Goth woman, so they left the store hand-in-hand, all in black.

Cosima loved putting order on chaos. She'd started so for the store, and she was just about ready to put order on chaos for the rest of her life.

Was LocalPharm her heart's desire? She wasn't sure. But she loved living up to her name. She'd start there.

Maybe she should thank Cupid.

Nah. She'd be happy about what she had accomplished and leave any thankyous for next year.

That was her real heart's desire.

A MULTI-GENRE FICTION WRITER, Johanna Rothman writes about intelligent people who create—or encounter trouble. Regardless of how they find themselves in trouble, these characters find solutions—often in imaginative ways. In addition to her short story collections, she has published short stories in *Pulphouse Fiction Magazine*, *Fiction River*, and *Holiday Spectaculars*.

An award-winning author of twenty nonfiction books about managing product development, Johanna incorporates humor—not just practicality—into her nonfiction. All because life is too short to take *too* seriously.

See her newsletters and all her writing at https://jrothman.com and https://createadaptablelife.com.

Two Valentine's
At Murphy's

By M.D. Posey

"Oh, my God. Craig?" Jennifer brought her shopping cart to a halt in the middle of the cereal aisle. A moment she'd both dreaded and wanted for over fifteen years, and never thought would happen, was here. She wondered if she could turn and run before he spotted her.

Instead, she found herself prompting him again. "Craig?"

Craig's head snapped up and turned toward her. His expression was blank. His gaze flitted over her face, then his brow furrowed.

For a moment, Jennifer thought she was wrong, that this wasn't him. A small part of her hoped it wasn't.

Only, his green eyes were as warm as she remembered.

His jaw went slack and his eyes wide. He drew in a sharp breath. "Jenny?"

They stared at each other, smiles tugging at the corners of their mouths, while Jennifer's guts tied themselves in knots.

Craig broke the silence. "Jenny Smithers!" He stepped toward her and drew her into an embrace.

She felt the muscles of his chest flex against her.

He broke the embrace quickly.

"It's Hanna now, actually. Jenn Hannah." She couldn't force the smile from her face. If only her guts would settle down.

Craig shook his head. "I'm...stunned.

He still got tongue-tied, talking to her.

God, are his shoulders even broader?

His gaze flickered over her shoulder. "I haven't been in here hardly at all since back in the day. There's good memories here. Mostly."

Their gazes came briefly together. Jenn looked away. Old regrets washed over her. "Yeah, last time we talked, we weren't very nice to each other, were we?"

Before Craig could answer, another shopper stopped in front of him. She bounced on her toes and clapped her hands. "Oh my gawd! Do you know who you are?!"

Craig looked from her to Jenn and back. His cheeks turned red as he focused on the young woman. "Pretty sure I do. Think I need to check my ID?"

The girl stepped closer, rested her hands on his forearm, and giggled as though he'd told the funniest joke she'd ever heard.

Craig glanced at Jenn again, clearly embarrassed.

Jenn clamped down on her displeasure at being interrupted. She focused on the seat of her grocery cart, pretending to read the text embossed in the plastic. Her irritation surprised her. Why should it bother her?

"Would you sign this, please?" More giggles followed. A few moments later, "Can I get a selfie with you?"

Jenn wondered if this was ever going to end.

She heard the camera shutter, then Craig said, "How'd it come out?"

The girl squealed. "It's great! Thank you so much!"

Jenn looked up in time to see the young woman scamper around the corner at the end of the aisle. When Jenn's gaze fell back on Craig, he was studying the back of a cereal box he'd pulled off the shelf. His face had grown quite red.

With the opportunity to tease him, she felt her irritation dissipate. "What was *that*?"

He dropped the cereal box into the basket at his feet and took a deep breath. "Sorry about that." He peeled off his ball cap and ran a hand through his blond hair, then tugged the cap back into place. "My adoring public."

"Your what?"

He cocked his head. "I just got traded to the Black Hawks?" When she didn't respond, he added, "It was front page news in the sports section for a couple of days here."

She had seen the articles, but she couldn't bring herself to admit it. "You can't seriously believe I follow hockey, can you?"

"After all this time, I thought maybe..."

She pursed her lips and shook her head.

"Anyway…" He picked the box of Captain Crunch out of the basket.

He just looked so adorable, holding the cereal box. A little kid who can't have what he wants. Add to that the broad shoulders, and the man the teenager had become.

He probably still has a nice ass, too. The realization descended on her, much to her chagrin. She was still attracted to him!

He set the cereal box on the shelf, "I was just thinking about breaking my summer training diet."

Still shocked, Jenn reached for an old standard. "Did you know diet is an acronym? Stands for 'Did I Eat That?'"

He nodded sharply. "Nice one."

This was veering off-course from the friendly, let-bygones-be-bygones reunion she usually pictured. "So...if you got traded to the Blackbirds—"

"Black *Hawks*," he corrected.

"Right. If you got traded to them, what are you doing *here*?"

"My wife and I are staying with my mom and dad until we can find a house, far enough from Chicago to be private, but close enough so it's an easy drive to the arena."

Of course, he's married. Why wouldn't he be? Keeping the dismay off her face, Jenn smiled and spread her arms. "Perfect. I'm a realtor."

Craig shook his head. "Sorry, my wife's already found a realtor. They're out looking now."

"Where are you guys looking?"

He shrugged. "She's looking. I don't really have the time to look at houses. Besides, Melody's got much better taste than me. She'll find three or four she really likes, then I'll see just those."

"How is it you have time for grocery shopping and autographs then, hmm? Mister spoiled athlete has somebody to do everything for him?"

Again, the self-conscious embarrassment, almost the big toe in the sand routine. "Not really."

"Yeah, yeah. You probably drive that lime green Lamborghini I saw in the parking lot."

When he cleared his throat, jammed his hands in his pockets and studied the floor, Jenn gaped. "Oh my God!"

His green eyes sparkled with amusement from beneath his brow. "One of the perks of being well paid."

"I guess, hey?" She took a deep breath and let it out slowly, amazed at how quickly they'd fallen into the same, comfortable, fifteen-year-old banter. "Well, I suppose I should let you get back to your—" She glanced in the empty basket near his feet. "Shopping?"

He peered into her cart. "Luckily, I don't need any bacon."

She lifted her chin. "My...husband's, not mine." Why did she hesitate before mentioning Karl?

The old, mischievous glint appeared in his eyes. "Sure, sure. Whatever you say."

She glanced down at the empty basket. "Hey, you're the one with the children's cereal craving. You only put it back because I caught you." She had always enjoyed teasing him.

He shook his head, amused. "I mostly came in to get one of those heart-shaped boxes of chocolate and a card for Melody."

Speaking her name seemed to stifle the mood. Their gazes met again and they both smiled but it felt forced compared to a moment ago. So did the hug that followed.

As they pulled apart, he caught her elbows. "It was great to see you again, Jenny."

She made herself smile. "You, too. It's been far too long."

He stepped back. "It has, for sure. Once we're in our new place, you and your hubby should come for dinner."

That was not a road she wanted to go down. If the four of them ever got together for dinner, Karl might miss it but Melody would pick up on her attraction to Craig immediately. Now the twisting in Jenn's gut was back.

Jenn stepped behind her cart and gripped the handle. Tight. "Karl and I would love that," she lied. "Give me a call, we'll set something up." She moved the cart past Craig, toward the end of the aisle. She didn't dare look back.

"Happy Valentine's Day," he said as she moved around the same corner his young, squealy fan had gone around.

JENN POPPED THE TRUNK AS she approached with her cart. She had hoped the anxious churning would ebb after she left Craig. But she could still feel it as she stuffed the grocery bags into the trunk.

She was surprised to discover she was disappointed because he hadn't fawned over her like he used to. He did still get tongue-tied, but really, it had been fifteen years since they'd seen each other. He wasn't going to fall all over himself. He was buying chocolates and a Valentine's card for his wife, for Christ's sake.

What kind of stupid name is Melody, anyway?

She slammed the case of bottled water into the trunk and reached up to grab the lid.

"Now those water bottles are going to fizz when you open them."

She froze. She'd hoped to get out of here before he got to the parking lot. She smiled nervously. "I promise, I'll be careful when I open them." She shut the trunk and turned to face him.

He wore the mischievous look that meant he was about to give someone a hard time.

"You gave me all that static about my Lambo, yet you drive a bright red Mercedes convertible? Can I start calling you pot? Or would kettle be better?"

She glanced at her car. Reluctance rose in her again. "Karl bought it for me. For our anniversary."

"Nice gift. What's *Karl* do?"

She felt an almost overwhelming need to get away. This was not what she wanted to talk about and she fought to maintain a civil, friendly exterior. "He's a divorce attorney."

"Of course." There was that look again, mischief. "A realtor and a divorce attorney? You must have awesome conversations at the dinner table."

She wouldn't encourage his teasing. "We've had some doozies, for sure."

"Mind if I ask a question?"

"Sure."

"You happy? Life's worked out like you wanted?"

What kind of a question was that? Did that mean he still cared for her? Or that he wanted to rub her face in it? Still maintaining the calm, she shrugged. "Mostly. There's always bumps in the road but..."

"Yeah, I can relate."

Jenn steeled herself as she glanced at the back of the car and ran a finger along one edge. There was a chance they would run into each other in the future. She preferred a clean slate. "Listen, I, uh..."

The awkward silence built before Jenn took a deep breath and blurted, "Our pizza place is still just across the street. Want to get a drink?"

He glanced across the street. The *Murphy's Pizza* sign was visible. "I'd love to but I can't. I've got a training session to get to. No rest for the wicked."

She kept the smile on her face. "Right. Of course. Good." She swallowed thickly and could feel the heat rising up her face. "Craig, I'm sorry I overreacted."

He furrowed his brow. "Overreacted?"

"When we were...involved."

When he still didn't seem to understand, she indicated the grocery store. "In the fridge." Her heart pounded. All this time she'd spent fretting about it, regretting it, and he didn't remember?

He glanced at the store over his shoulder. "Really? Are you kidding me?"

"It needed to be said. Wipe the slate clean."

His gaze held hers. "What is it they say? 'Takes two to tango?' We were *both* young and stupid back then."

Relief flooded her. "Well, you need to get to training and I need to get my groceries home. It was good to see you, Craig."

She blipped the lock open and the horn honked. She yanked the door handle but it was still locked. She frowned and blipped it and the horn honked again. When she yanked on the door again, it was still locked.

She glanced at Craig.

Amusement shone in his eyes. "Having trouble?"

She scowled at the key fob and then rolled her eyes. "Think it would help if I pushed the unlock button instead of the lock button?"

"Possibly." Craig rested a hand on her elbow. "You okay?"

She brushed hair from her forehead, moving her elbow out of his grip. "Yeah, sorry. I'm distracted. Big deal's about to close. Just waiting to hear. Always seems like it takes forever to happen."

He stepped back. "Alright then. Good luck on that deal. I'll talk to you later."

"You bet," she forced herself to say cheerily.

He strode toward the green Lamborghini and blipped the lock open as he walked. She watched as he grasped the passenger door handle and it arced up.

Still does have a nice ass, that's for sure.

He set the box of chocolates on the seat and reached up to throw the door shut. As he moved around to the driver's side, he glanced up and saw her watching.

She waved awkwardly and hurried into her own car. She watched in the rearview mirror as he pulled out of his parking space and surged by, his tinted windows not letting her to see him one last time.

Once he was out of sight, she realized she was sitting with her keys clenched in her hand so tightly her knuckles were white.

She started the car and shook her head, suddenly feeling foolish. She met her own gaze in the rearview mirror.

Jesus Christ, Jennifer. Get ahold of yourself. The two of you aren't kids anymore.

And they *had* been kids, back then…

"Price check on till four. Price check on till four. Heinz ketchup, twenty-four ounce bottle."

It was her first day on the job, and Jennifer already hated the ugly and uncomfortable polyester uniform. It made her self-conscious as hell. Speaking over the intercom only made that feeling worse. Her voice was squeaky. She sounded like a twelve-year-old, not sixteen. She hoped the guys checking the prices could tell what she'd said.

The woman training Jennifer rested a hand on her shoulder. "Set the ketchup aside for now and keep ringing things through. One of the guys will be up with the price in a minute."

Jenn glanced nervously at the customer in front of her. The customer gave a thin-lipped smile back.

A guy in the male version of the scratchy uniform rushed up and skidded to a halt by the till. He stared at Jenn, open-mouthed.

The woman training Jenn grinned. When the guy didn't speak, she said, "Earth to Craig, Earth to Craig. Come in, Craig."

Someone in line at Jenn's till snickered.

Craig blinked. "Um... what?"

The training woman prompted him. "You have the price for the ketchup?"

Craig frowned. "Yeah, it's... it's... Shit, I forgot!"

"Mr. MacAllister! Watch your language."

"Sorry, ma'am... uh, ma'ams," Craig said to the women in the line. They were trying to not laugh and failing.

Craig's embarrassed gaze fell on Jenn. He said to the training woman, "I'll be right back." He rushed away.

Jenn return to ringing through the woman's groceries, the afterimage of the cute guy playing in her mind making her cheeks warm.

A different uniformed guy rushed up. His nametag said 'Douglas'. "Eighty-nine cents."

Jenn quashed her disappointment that the cute guy had sent someone else to give her the price. "The ketchup?"

The guy blinked. "Yeah. Eighty-nine cents."

Jenn punched in the eighty-nine cents, and stuffed the ketchup into the customers bag. She glanced over her shoulder as Douglas hurried away.

He's not as cute as Clark... Chris... Craig! That was his name. *Have to keep an eye out for him.*

She wondered if they went to the same school. She didn't recognize him but that didn't mean anything. Starting high school in a new town had meant a month of new faces. She couldn't remember them all.

Over the next few months, Jenn hoped to have an actual conversation with Craig instead of pleasantries surrounding price checks. It seemed as though he was always rushing off after work. She'd watched him punching out, snatching his coat up and dashing for the exit.

Where did he go in such a hurry? She hadn't been able to ask him because he was always in a rush to leave.

Christmas came and went. As winter moved through January, Craig could almost look her in the eyes when they spoke. It was cute. So was he.

February arrived, and Jenn still didn't have a date for Valentine's Day, when everyone at school was boasting about *their* dates. It was humiliating.

Valentine's Day was a Saturday, so she didn't have to endure endless teasing about her lack of a date that night.

Patty, who worked with Jenn at the grocery store, asked if she wanted to go hang out at Murphy's Pizza, instead.

Jenn jumped at the chance to get out of the house on a Saturday night, especially *this* Saturday night. Patty picked Jenn up in her mom's car. It was unseasonably warm for the middle of February, so Jenn wore only a camisole under her coat, her tightest jeans, and her favorite heels. She left her ash-blonde hair loose about her shoulders.

Once they were seated in Murphy's, Jenn glanced around the room. It was almost nine o'clock, and the crowd had thinned, but there were still many diners.

After they'd got their pops, Jenn took another look around the room, slower this time. At almost every table was a couple.

But at a table in the back corner was Douglas whats-his-name, of the eighty-nine cent ketchup. He was also there with someone, for a half-empty glass and an open menu were on the table opposite him. Douglas waved when she caught his gaze.

She smiled awkwardly and studied the menu. When she dared to look up again, Douglas' friend had returned.

Douglas smiled at Jenn, this time.

His somebody else turned around.

Craig.

The butterflies in Jenn's stomach sprang to life. They got worse when Douglas and Craig headed in her direction. Craig's gaze locked on her.

Why wasn't he as shy here as he was at work? *I hope that continues.*

"All of Rome is here," he quipped.

Clearly, that was supposed to be witty. She gripped her hands together under the table. "Where else would we be?"

Douglas said, "Funny you should ask. We have two empty chairs at our table. Would you care to be over there?"

The butterflies got even worse. Jenn glanced at Patty, who looked as if she was on the verge of rolling her eyes.

"Sure, why not?" Patty said.

As they were gathering their things, the waitress stopped by. "You moving to sit with them?" she said to Jenn.

"Is that okay?"

"It's my table, too."

"Thanks, Rachel," Craig said. "We'll make sure there's a little something in your pay tonight."

Rachel's smile was warm. Too warm. "Damn well better be."

Jenn frowned as they walked toward the table. "You know her?" It sounded more accusatory than she had meant it to be.

"She's dating my older brother," Craig said.

The relief Jenn felt surprised her.

At the boys' table, Craig pulled out the chair next to him.

"Thank you." She fought the urge to gush as she sat. She put her chin on her fist and studied him.

He was in great shape and he had a really nice ass. That didn't hurt at all but even more than the physique, she liked that with everyone else he was strong and confident but around her, he went all gaga.

"Jennifer?" Patty had reached across the table to touch her hand.

"Sorry, what?"

Rachel, the waitress, was standing with pen poised over her notepad. "What'll you have?"

Jenn turned to Craig. "What are you having?"

"Medium pepperoni and mushroom."

"If you made that a large, we could split it."

He seemed pleasantly surprised. "Done." He turned to Rachel. "Can you make that a large, please?"

Rachel chuckled. "I can definitely do that."

Jenn watched Rachel walk away. "What's with her?"

"Oh, my brother is going to tease me endlessly about splitting my pizza with a girl, now that his girlfriend knows about it."

Jenn worried that he wouldn't want to spend time with her if it was going to cause him problems. "I could have ordered something else."

"Thanks, but it's too late. She already knows. Besides, it's a pretty good reason to get teased."

A warm glow radiated through her. "Well then, here's to you getting teased endlessly."

"I'll drink to that." He raised his glass. They clinked them together.

Patty made a face. "You guys are gross."

"Tell me about it," Doug said. "So sweet, we won't need dessert."

"Got that right." In a high voice, Patty sang, "Oh, Dougie, I loves you whole big bunches." She made noisy kissing sounds.

They both laughed while Craig and Jenn stared at them.

"Just ignore them," Craig advised Jenn. "Leave them to their kissy face sounds. We'll have a normal, grown-up conversation."

Jenn leaned toward him, and rested her hand on his forearm. "What shall we talk about? I know. Where do you always rush off to, after work?"

He shrugged, looking self-conscious again. "Home to bed. Curfew is ten o'clock."

"Curfew? Are your parents that strict?"

"Not my parents. My coach."

"Your what?"

"My coach. He says I have a real chance at being drafted in two years, if I do all the right things, like getting enough sleep every night."

She narrowed her eyes. "I see. Wouldn't another of those *right things* be doing well in school?"

"You bet."

"But you're never there. You didn't drop out or something like that, did you?"

Douglas chirped, "Are you kidding? Mr. Academic High Achiever over here drop out? Not a chance."

Craig rolled his eyes. "I go to New Trier High."

Jenn frowned. "Where's that?"

"Winnetka."

"Why would you go all the way up there?"

"It's not *that* far away and they have the best high school hockey program in the state."

"You go all that way just to play hockey?"

Craig clutched at his chest. "You're not a hockey fan?"

She wondered if she had just spoiled everything. "Not even a little bit," she confessed.

"Have you ever been to a game?"

"No."

"Would you come and watch me play?" He indicated the two across from them. "Doug and Patty'll come with you. Won't you, guys?"

Jenn was thankful Rachel showed up with their food, which covered the awkward pause in the conversation. .

Rachel set everything on the table and made sure everyone's drinks were good, while no one said a word.

After Rachel had gone, Jenn tried to recover the mood. She smiled at Craig, leaned in, and rubbed her shoulder against his. "I guess I could be talked into watching a game."

That set off Douglas and Patty again.

"Oh Jenny," Douglas mocked with a falsetto voice, "will you please, please, please come watch me play hockeyball?"

Patty put a hand to her chest. "But Craigy, I don't like the hockeyball. Can't we just make out, instead?"

Jenn swatted at Patty with her napkin. "Shut up!"

Douglas and Patty laughed.

Craig said softly to Jenn, "Don't worry about hockey. We'll find something else to talk about." He reached for a piece of pizza and took a big bite.

Jenn breathed an inward sigh of relief.

After Valentine's Day, the two of them became regulars at Murphy's. When they both worked the evening shift, they always came over to eat afterward. Same meal every time, a large pepperoni and mushroom and two pops.

It got so that when they walked in the door, the cook would put their pizza together and have it in the oven by the time they sat down.

If Craig had to practice the next morning, they would get their pizza to go, and he would drop Jenn at home. He always came inside to say hello to her parents.

They were very impressed with Craig. He could talk with them using more than the monosyllables most teenagers managed.

One night when Craig pulled up to the curb in front of her house, only the outdoor lights were on. Inside, the house was dark.

He looked at his watch and then back at the house. "It's too early for your parents to be in bed. Did they go out?"

"Sort of. They went to a convention in Florida for my dad's work. They won't be back until Sunday night."

"You don't mind staying in that big house all by yourself for five days? Isn't it creepy?"

"It's fine. I like the quiet."

"Alright then. I guess I'll see you at work tomorrow?"

"You're not coming in?"

He shrugged. "No mom and dad for me to come say hi to."

"Would you at least walk me to the door?"

He looked at his watch again. "I guess I've got a few minutes."

"Look, if you really don't want to –"

"No, no. It's fine." He slid the car into park and shut the engine off.

Together, they strolled up the driveway and around to the back of the house. The casualness of Jenn's stride did not match the anxious roiling of her stomach.

At the back door, she fished out her keys and unlocked it. Then she opened it, reached inside to turn on the light, and stepped aside so Craig could go in.

He opened his mouth to speak, then closed it and stepped into the house.

The usual pile of shoes were on the mat beside the door. Three steps led up to the kitchen.

"You want me to do a walk through?" Craig asked. "Make sure no bad guys are lurking in the dark? No monsters under the bed?" He had a teasing smile.

Jenn stood with her back against the door and flipped the deadbolt shut. With a nervous smile, she took two steps to where he stood.

She didn't hesitate. She wound her arms around his neck and kissed him. Hard.

When she broke the kiss, he said, "Jenny, I…"

"Shut up." She pressed her lips to his again.

It seemed to her that he wasn't sure what was happening, or how far she intended this to go.

Their kiss grew far more heated when she thrust her tongue into his mouth. Yet he was still being tentative.

When she slid her hand down his torso, over his belt, to caress the hard bulge beneath, it was as though she'd flipped a switch—for both of them. They scrabbled frantically at each other's clothing. Those ugly polyester uniforms had never looked so good to Jenn, strewn about the back door landing.

She stifled a giggle when he fumbled with the back of her bra. After a couple of tugs, she stopped him, then undid the catch between her breasts.

When they were naked, she nudged him backward so his calves ran into the bottom step. One more nudge and his ass dropped to the next step.

She met his lustful gaze. "You have to pull out." Then she straddled him and lowered herself onto him. As their coupling moved from excited to frenzied, his hands scrabbled at her hips, trying to lift her off. She clamped down harder, too caught up in it. She wanted to feel him pulse and jerk inside her.

When they were basking in the afterglow, he said, "I'm sorry, I–"

She cut him off with a kiss. "Nothing to be sorry about."

Once they were dressed again, Jenn kissed him good night and nuzzled him before he slipped out the door. She didn't want him to go. She wanted him to spend the night.

It seemed more romantic than him driving home to sleep in his own bed.

But if he didn't go home, his parents would freak out. And besides, Patty would phone soon, demanding details about how the evening had gone.

Jenn wanted to gush about Craig so much, Patty would be in a sugar coma by the end of the call.

When she had given Patty the details, Jenn finished with a contented sigh.

After a moment's silence, Patty said, "Good for you, Jenn. I'm glad you guys were able to go from friends to…what? Boyfriend and girlfriend?"

"I don't know. I mean, I guess so. What else would we be?"

That night, Jenn slept deeply. Everything was right with the world.

The four days before Jenn's parents got home were glorious. They made love six more times. Twice in her bed, twice on the sofa in the living room, once in the shower, and even once on the kitchen table.

Jenn hoped her parents wouldn't notice the glow she wore, which Patty had pointed out. Also the way Jenn floated as she walked.

The first night after her parents had returned, Craig drove Jenn home and walked up the driveway with her as usual. He paused to hug and kiss her before they went inside. He whispered in her ear, "These last five days have been great, Jenny. I'm going to miss being friends with benefits. I hope your parents go away again soon."

Jenn's heart stopped for a couple of beats. She felt the blood drain from her face.

Her parents were waiting for them to come into the house. She didn't want them to think there was something wrong and start grilling her about it.

And Craig was waiting for her reply.

It all ran through Jenn's mind as they were pulling apart. So she forced a smile. "Totally, me too. For sure." It came out wooden.

She turned to the door, fumbling for her keys. It was all she could do to not let the façade crumble while Craig did his normal five minute conversation with her mom and dad.

Once he was gone, she rushed to her bedroom, closed the door, and collapsed onto her bed, muffling her sobs with a pillow.

It was a long and sleepless night.

FOUR DAYS LATER, JENN WORKED the same shift as Craig. She had not spoken to him since the night her parents had returned. She avoided looking around. She didn't want to glimpse him. It would just make her angry and sad.

She focused on the customers instead.

The evening crawled by. After what seemed like hours, Jenn looked at her watch and found that only thirty minutes had passed.

When she looked up, Craig was walking up the aisle, straight toward her.

He smiled. "Hey stranger! Where've you been hiding?"

She met his gaze, her hand clenched by her hip. "Just been busy."

He seemed surprised. "Okay, then..."

A customer wheeled her cart up to Jenn's till and unloaded.

Relieved, Jenn turned to attend to the groceries moving along the belt toward her.

When she'd finished with the customer and looked up, Craig had gone. She didn't see him for the rest of her shift. When she punched out, he was waiting by the employee entrance.

"Ready for pizza?" he asked.

How can he not know? She kept her school books and coat between her and him. She couldn't meet his eyes. "I can't tonight. I have to get home."

"Why?"

Her anger was building. She met his gaze. "I just...I have to get home."

"Fine. We'll get our pizza to go."

She wished he would just drop it, but knew he wouldn't. "I'm not in the mood for pizza tonight."

"Okay. I'll just give you a ride home."

She slumped inwardly. A ride home would start the conversation she most wanted to avoid. Her voice quavered as she said, "My dad's waiting in the parking lot."

Craig was silent.

She risked looking at him . He looked as if he'd been punched in the gut. "Jenny, what the hell's going on? It's like —"

Another employee was heading for the exit. Once the door closed, Craig spoke *sotto voce*. "It's like you're trying to avoid me. And I haven't done anything wrong."

She couldn't answer. The lump in her throat cut off all her words. She turned her back to him so he wouldn't see the tears threatening to spill down her cheeks.

"Jenny, just talk to me. We can work it out, no matter what the problem is."

The second admission in as many minutes that he had no idea. No clue. She swallowed thickly, her heart pounding. "I don't think we should see each other anymore." It came out in a rush, barely above a whisper.

"*Excuse me?*" He was almost shouting. "*Why?*"

His barking removed her reticence, but she wouldn't do this out here. She grabbed the lapel of his jacket, and pulled him across the room to the nearest commercial refrigerator. She yanked it open and stalked inside.

He must have seen the fury in her eyes, for he took a step back.

"You wanna talk?" she raged, "Fine! Get in here and shut the fucking door."

He almost looked scared. "Jenny, I—"

"In here!" She thrust her index finger downward.

Anger colored his face. He strode into the fridge and slammed the door.

They could both see their breath in the air.

Craig was shaking. Jenn didn't think it was from the cold.

He stepped closer. "Y'know, I don't know what your problem is but –"

"*My* problem? Are you fucking kidding me?"

"Yes, your problem! What is it? You fucked me half-a-dozen times, and now you're ready to move on to the next guy?"

Jenn was aghast. Her mouth dropped open in shock. "Oh my God! This was such a fucking mistake! I will regret those five days for the rest of my life!"

"What the hell is that supposed to mean?"

"Friends with benefits?" she screeched.

"Yeah. Weren't we just –"

"Friends with benefits!? The only benefit you're ever going to get from me, MacAllister, is me not kicking your fucking nuts hard enough they get stuck up your nose!"

"That's all this could ever be. Coach says I could get drafted in the next year. I could end up half-way across the country. I thought you knew that."

She tried to leave. He didn't grab her arm to stop her, but did move into her path. "Jenny, surely we can work –"

She held up a hand to silence him. She stalked to the door and slammed her hand against the release. It burst open, hitting the shelving unit beside it.

She paused in the doorway and looked at him. "I'm only going to say this once. Fuck. Off."

She stormed out the employee entrance to her dad's car. She had a lot of explaining to do, but first she cried all the way home.

She never saw Craig again.

JENN SAT IN ONE OF the Adirondack chairs on her front verandah and sipped that first soul-restoring mouthful of fresh coffee, enjoying the warm spring morning. The sun had been up for an hour. It bathed the south-facing verandah with bright, warm sunshine. She would have to shade her iPad to see the screen properly.

She had finished scrolling through the Google Newsfeed when Karl strolled out, carrying his own coffee. He set the cup on the arm of the other chair, then moved over to the mailbox hanging on the verandah's white railing and retrieved the day's issue of the *Chicago Tribune*.

Jenn rolled her eyes. "When are you going to give up that archaic way of getting the news?"

Karl glanced at her as he sat and opened the paper. He gave it a snap to straighten it out, and peered at her over the drooping corner. "Can't do *that* with an iPad."

Jenn barely heard him over the pounding of her heart.

She stared open-mouthed at the headline on the front page:

WIFE OF BLACK HAWKS STAR CENTER IN HORRIFIC ACCIDENT
Melody MacAllister not expected to survive.

She couldn't imagine the state Craig must be in. Her heart ached for him.

Karl frowned at her. "What're you looking at?" He turned the paper to read the headline. "Since when do you give two hoots about hockey?"

She swallowed thickly and shrugged. "Craig MacAllister worked at Matherson's at the same time I did. Back when we were in high school."

Karl grunted in acknowledgement and tipped his head back so he could read the article through the glasses perched on the end of his nose.

"How many times have I told you that if you push the glasses up, reading will be much easier?"

He tsked. "Says here, she's in Holy Cross Hospital on life support. The family's asking for privacy during this difficult time."

"That's terrible. I hate to think what Craig is going through."

Karl raised an eyebrow at her over the top of the paper. "The team chartered him a private plane last night to get him back home. Must be nice. Regular folks would have to throw themselves on the mercy of the airlines."

"One of the perks of being well paid," Jenn muttered. Could she help Craig without giving anything away?

Her iPad dinged. Jenn thumbed it open. It was a message from Douglas Burke, from high school. Jenn couldn't remember if she'd known his last name before.

Hi Jennifer,

Long time, no see. I hope you're well. Have you heard about Craig's wife? I'm getting ahold of a few people from back in the day. Thinking we could go to the hospital, see how he's holding up and if there's anything we can do. If you'd like to come, we're meeting just inside the main entrance of Holy Cross at 7:00 tonight. Hope to see you there.

Doug

Karl leaned over to peer at the iPad. "Who's that from?"

Jenn smiled, nostalgic. "Douglas Burke. Used to work at Matherson's. Was a year ahead of me in high school, same as Craig."

Karl grunted. "What's he want?"

She shrugged, acting casual. "The group from high school are going to go to the hospital tonight. See if there's anything they can do to help Craig. Douglas was wondering if I wanted to go."

"You gonna go?"

"It *would* be nice to see the old gang. It's been ages."

"Do me a favor while you're there? Take my Black Hawks jersey with you and get him to sign it?"

"You're kidding, right? His wife is on life support and you want me to get his autograph?" She thought of the squealy schoolgirl in the cereal aisle.

"Might not get another chance."

Irritated at Karl's selfishness, Jenn crossed her arms. "I'll invite him for dinner once this is over. You can get whatever you want signed then."

Karl snapped his newspaper and went back to reading. "Deal."

She rolled her eyes and got to her feet, headed for the front door. "I've got an open house I've got to get ready for," she threw over her shoulder as she stepped inside.

He turned the page. "Don't forget I've got that deposition in Delaware. You're taking me to the airport this afternoon," he called after her.

JENN STOOD TO ONE SIDE of the Holy Cross Hospital entrance. The knots in her stomach were back. She wasn't sure if it was because she was going to see Craig again or because of what might happen while she was here.

She recognized Douglas and Patty when they came through the doors. They both lit up when they saw her.

Jenn's eyes brimmed with tears as they group hugged.

"I'm glad you came," Doug said. "Craig will be pleased. When's the last time you two saw each other?"

"I ran into him in Matherson's a couple months ago. It was...sort of awkward but mostly friendly." She shrugged. "It was Valentine's Day. He was buying a box of chocolates for…"

"Melody," Douglas supplied.

Jenn nodded. "Right. We talked for a bit in the aisle and then a bit later in the parking lot."

Patty grinned, teasing. "And...?"

Jenn feigned disinterest. "Too much water under that bridge."

Patty focused on Douglas. "Have you heard how she's doing?"

"If the doctors are to be believed, not good." When both of them looked inquisitive, he continued. "Craig called me last night. He's just barely keeping it together."

"I can imagine." Jenn shuddered.

"Ready to go up?" Doug asked.

"No one else is coming?"

"Like always, it's just the four of us."

No one else was in the elevator with them.

"By the way," Doug said, "the password to get past security is 'Matherson's'"

"*Password?*" Jenn repeated.

"They just want to make sure fans can't get in."

The elevator dinged as the doors opened. They moved down the hall to where a security guard stood in front of the door to a private ward. He held up his hand as they approached. "I'm sorry but this area's off-limits to the public."

Douglas peered at the guard's badge. "Thanks, Tony. Can you let Mr. MacAllister know the people from Matherson's are here?"

The guard looked them over. Jenn smiled to encourage the guard to let them in.

He grabbed the mic near his collar. "This is Tony. I've got three people from Matherson's out here."

Jenn looked eagerly over the guard's shoulder. She saw Craig appear in the window. He glanced to his right and said something. The guard's radio squawked with an all-clear and he stepped to the side and pressed the door open, holding it for them as they passed.

Craig embraced each of them in turn. He looked awful. Disheveled, unshaven, red-rimmed eyes. Defeated. "Thanks for coming, guys. I really appreciate it. It's tough sitting here alone."

Jenn was suddenly very glad they came. "Where's your mom and dad? Where's your brother?"

"What about Melody's family?" Patty added.

Craig stuffed his hands in his pockets. "Mel's an only child. Her parents were gone before we met. My mom and dad are on holidays in Italy. And David lives in Hawaii."

Douglas blew a breath out and ran his fingers through his hair. "Man, you shoulda told me that last night. I'da come and sat with you."

"I would have, too," Jenn said.

"Me, too," Patty added.

Craig shrugged. "Wanted to spend some time alone with her." He stared blankly through the window into Melody's room, eyes brimming with tears. "The machines are keeping her alive." He heaved a great, shaky sigh. "That drunk's car plowed right into the driver's door. She never had a chance."

Jenn rubbed his arm as a tear cascaded down his cheek. She hated seeing him like this.

"I'm just waiting for Mom, Dad, and David to get here. Our lawyer has already given the hospital Mel's DNR." He shrugged. "Not really much to do but sit."

Jenn felt a grin tugging at the corners of her mouth. It would be so inappropriate to start to giggle right now. She tried to tamp it down as she cleared her throat. "And yet, here we are, *standing* in the hallway."

Craig looked at her blankly.

"Come on, then. Let's sit." She took Craig by the arm and led him toward the alcove full of chairs outside Melody's room. Douglas and Patty followed and they each sank into a chair.

"So when's everyone supposed to get here?" Douglas leaned forward to see around Patty.

Craig drew in a deep, shuddering breath. "David will be late tomorrow night. Last time I talked to my dad, he said they were on stand-by with the airlines and they'd call me as soon as they knew something."

"That could take days." Jenn put her arm around Craig's shoulders. "And you're okay with keeping her alive like that until then?"

He shrugged. "What else can I do?"

Jenn focused on the pattern in the carpet and tried to put as much concern in her voice as possible. "You said the hospital's already got Melody's DNR. You could," she caught his gaze, "say goodbye. Tonight. If you want." She hated that the waiting was tearing him apart.

He looked into Melody's room. Jenn couldn't see her from where they sat but she thought she understood. Her heart ached with the pain he was feeling. He was clearly not ready to say goodbye.

Who would be?

Jenn worried that the longer he left it, the harder it would be, even with his family here.

"I know that's the moment, the choice I'm facing." He shook his head. "But right now, I can't even imagine it...even though that's the only outcome."

Jenn didn't envy him. While Craig stared blankly into Melody's room, the three of them sat quietly.

"You were right, Jenny," the voice on the phone said.

Jenn sat up, groggy with sleep, and peered at the digital clock on top of the chest of drawers across the room. "Craig?"

"Yeah..."

"It's almost one o'clock in the morning."

"Yeah."

"You want to say goodbye now?"

"It's time."

"Why are you phoning me?"

"I don't know if I can do it alone."

"What about the guys on your team?"

"Played in Anaheim last night. L.A. tomorrow. Then they have to get ready for the playoffs."

Jenn scrubbed her fingers through her hair. "What about Douglas? Or Patty?"

"If you don't want to come, Jenny, just say so. I can get –"

Jenn sat up straight. "No, it's fine. I'll be there as quick as I can."

Slightly more than an hour later, Jenn charged up to the hospital. She didn't want Craig to go through this alone, either.

Craig was waiting there with the guard to let her in.

The moment she was inside, they hugged.

Craig looked exhausted as he leaned against the wall of the elevator.

She anxiously watched the floor numbers count up, staring straight ahead. The higher they rode, the tenser Jenn got. She jumped when the elevator dinged at the top floor.

A different guard was in front of the ward door. He moved aside and held the door open for them.

There was a crowd of doctors and nurses in the room.

Jenn's upset grew at the sight of them. "I thought you said you didn't want to do this alone."

Craig looked at the medical team through the window. "They're just doctors and nurses. They don't know me. They aren't someone who it will mean something when they hold my hand. Someone I care about and who cares about me."

The lump in Jenn's throat grew. I have to be strong for him right now.

She took his hand in hers. "Okay, I'm holding your hand. Come on." She led him into the room. The medical staff fell silent. The only sounds were the beeping of the heart monitor and the hissing of the ventilator.

Craig squeezed Jenn's hand. Jenn's tears grew. Craig's pain was tearing at her.

A doctor eased to the other side of the bed. "Are you ready, Mr. MacAllister?"

Craig's chin quivered. He squeezed Jenn's hand as his tears spilled. They dripped onto Melody's hand and he wiped the tears away.

Jenn said, "I don't think he's ever going to answer 'Yes' to that question."

The doctor looked regretful. "Yeah, of course. He said he wanted to be the one to turn off the machine."

"What does he need to do?"

The doctor indicated the machine the ventilator hose was connected to and the lighted switch on the bottom right corner. "Just flip that switch."

"What'll happen?" Craig whispered.

The doctor said softy, "The machine will stop breathing for her, so her chest will stop rising and falling. Her heartbeat will become erratic and then it will stop."

"Will it hurt? Will she thrash around?"

The doctor shook his head. "She won't feel a thing."

Jenn saw that some of the nurses had tears in their eyes, too.

Craig turned to her. His chin quivered. "I can't..."

Jenn's chest constricted with unshed tears. "I know. I know." She put her arm around his shoulders.

"Can you...?"

Jenn gently shook her head. "It's the last loving thing you'll do for her."

"What?"

"Letting her go."

Tears slid down his cheeks. Craig looked from the switch to Melody's face and back. He took a deep breath. Then another. A third.

For a moment, Jenn thought he wasn't going to be able to do it.

Craig let go of her hand. He leaned over the bed and kissed Melody on the forehead. He straightened and put his hand on the switch.

He glanced at the heart monitor, beeping rhythmically. He looked at Jenn.

"It's okay, Craig. It's what she needs."

Craig studied Melody and without looking away from her, flipped the switch.

WHEN THE BLACK HAWKS WON the Stanley Cup two months later, many pundits gave the credit to Craig. He won the Conn Smythe Trophy for MVP of the playoffs. The press said he had played like a man possessed.

Jenn knew he was playing like a man in mourning. The playoffs had started two days after Craig had flicked that switch. Craig was front and center from the first game onward. She suspected he used his grief to fuel his play. A smart strategy, she supposed. Only, she didn't think it would help him grieve. It would just keep his grief alive.

Jenn watched on TV the parade for the Black Hawks and the big celebration downtown. It seemed as though the entire city of Chicago was in love with Craig. He got the loudest cheer when he was introduced. And an even louder cheer after his speech, where he dedicated his Conn Smythe win to his dear, departed wife.

In August, on Karl's birthday, everyone was on lawn chairs in the back yard, drinking beer and laughing together. Craig arrived with a team-signed jersey for Karl. He'd also brought the Stanley Cup.

The look on Karl's face was priceless as Jenn appeared on the back deck with the jersey and even more so when Craig strolled out with the cup.

Karl and his friends couldn't believe it. They spent the afternoon drinking beer from it. Craig just sat back with a funny little grin on his face the entire time, sipping bottled water.

Before he left, Craig gathered everyone around the cup for a group photo Jenn knew would become one of Karl's most treasured possessions. Craig shook hands with each of Karl's friends and gave Karl the biggest hug before he left.

Karl rated it his best birthday ever.

JENN STEPPED OUT ONTO THE front verandah with her precious first cup of coffee. The morning was clear and crisp, with a slight chill in the air. The leaves had started to turn. This was the time of year Jenn looked forward. The beauty of the yellows, oranges, and reds in the trees always left her feeling reverent and relaxed.

Jenn wrapped her mother's homemade quilt around herself, leaving the hand holding the coffee free. As she settled into one of the Adirondack chairs, Craig's gaudy Lamborghini pulled to a stop in front of the house.

The driver's door pivoted up and Craig climbed out, smiling.

Jenn smiled back. "When are you going to get a regular colored car?"

"I was thinking of getting a second one in, like, hot pink or something."

Jenn rolled her eyes. "Well, don't park it in front of my house."

"Fine. I won't." He bounded up on the steps. "Karl around?"

She nodded. "Just getting ready for work. Why?"

He reached into his inside jacket pocket. "Brought you guys two tickets for opening night. Box seats, right at center ice."

Karl burst through the screen door. "Box seats? Center ice? Oh man –"

He stopped. His face grew slack. He toppled forward. Karl landed heavily on the deck boards.

He didn't put his hands out, didn't protect himself at all.

"Karl!" Jenn rushed to him. "Karl?" She shook him to bring him around. No response. She tugged on his shoulder to turn him over but he was so much bigger than her, it was difficult and took her a moment or two. Then she realized Craig was on the phone.

"...thirty-five year old male, collapsed and unresponsive...starting CPR..." Craig handed her his phone.

She took it in a daze.

"Talk to the 911 operator. She'll need some information."

Craig tilted Karl's head to make sure his windpipe was open, and started chest compressions.

The EMTs showed up a few minutes later and despite several life-saving procedures, pronounced Karl dead, covered him with a blanket, and let Craig and Jenn know they'd inform the coroner.

That was the last thing Jenn was conscious of until the coroner's van pulled up in front of the house. She was sitting on the verandah steps, Craig beside her with his arm around her shoulders.

As the two occupants of the van strode up the footpath to the house, Craig nodded at them and then nudged Jenn.

Craig murmured to her, "Let's go inside and let these guys work."

Jenn let herself be led inside.

KARL'S FUNERAL WAS A SMALL affair. Family and close friends only.

Craig was seated at the back, behind everyone. Jenn stepped to the edge of the aisle so she could squeeze his hand as she and Karl's family moved up the aisle toward the casket.

After the funeral, family and friends were invited back to Jenn's house to celebrate Karl's life. Jenn's parents drove her home and got her settled on the Adirondack chair on the verandah. Jenn's mom ducked inside to check on the caterers, while her dad sat in the other chair.

When Craig's Lamborghini pulled to the curb, he looked up sharply. "What the heck is that?" He watched warily as Craig strode up the front walk and up the verandah steps.

Craig pulled off his sunglasses and stuck out his hand. "Mr. Smithers, how are you, sir?"

Her father took Craig's hand. "Do I know you, son?"

"Craig MacAllister, sir. I used to drive Jenny home from Matherson's when we were teenagers."

Her dad peered at him. "Oh, sure. Polite, friendly, and overly obsessed with hockey."

Craig smiled briefly. "That's me."

With more people coming up the front walk, Jenn's dad said, "Thanks for coming, son and excuse me. Gotta greet more well-wishers."

Craig squatted down next to Jenn's chair. "How you doin'?"

Jenn bit back the urge to implore him to take her away from all of this. Instead, she shrugged. "About like you'd expect."

He rested a hand on her forearm. "I know exactly what you mean." Their gazes locked for a moment and it seemed to Jenn he wanted to say more. He glanced over his shoulder. "I'm not going to stay."

Jenn felt more tears well. Karl was gone and now Craig was leaving. She wanted—*needed* him to stay. But she couldn't say anything. If she tried, the dam would burst. She gripped his arm hard and shook her head.

"If I stay, a bunch of his buddies will be focused on me," Craig said softly. "I don't want to distract anyone from celebrating Karl. I just wanted to make sure you're okay. I'll be in touch in a few days."

He kissed her on the cheek, stood up, slipped his sunglasses back on, and threaded his way through the people coming up the sidewalk, back to his car. When he raised the door, he looked up at Jenn and waved before ducking into the car and driving away.

She felt the most alone she'd ever felt in her life. The dam burst.

"COME ON, IT'LL BE LIKE old times," Patty said over the phone. "You and me at Murphy's for pizza on Valentine's Day."

Jenn scrunched her face up. "I don't know if I'm ready to be with people yet."

Patty's voice took on an authoritative tone. "You said the same thing at Christmas and you were fine."

"But that was at your house, not out in public."

"Too bad, I've already reserved a table. I'm picking you up in half an hour." Patty hung up.

When they got to Murphy's, the lineup was out the door. Jenn groaned. "Oh man, this is going to take forever."

"Nope, we have a reservation." Patty grabbed Jenn and drew her through the front door. Patty explained to the hostess about the reservation.

The hostess picked up two menus and led them through the loud and crowded restaurant. At the very back, a table for two sat in a private alcove. As they approached, Jenn could only see one chair and the front edge of the tabletop. The second chair was completely hidden from view.

"I never knew this was here. The table's almost cut off from the whole restaurant."

"I figured you wouldn't mind a bit of privacy," Patty said.

"You were right. Now we can relax and enjoy dinner."

"Great." Patty moved ahead of Jenn to pull out her chair. As Jenn stepped up to the table, Craig was sitting on the other side.

Her heart pounded. She fell into the other chair.

Patty kissed Jenn on the cheek. "Enjoy your dinner." she said, and left.

Jenn's eyes filled with tears as she watched Craig.

He sat forward, leaned his elbows on the table and caught her gaze. "Can I ask you a question?"

Jenn couldn't speak. She nodded.

"Will you be my valentine?"

Jenn covered her mouth as the tears flowed freely.

Craig held out his hand and she took it. When she was able to speak, her voice quavered. "How...*why* did you arrange all this?"

He wore a self-conscious grin that she knew well, though his eyes, too, were glistening with moisture. "I wanted to surprise you, so I got Patty to help me."

She cleared her throat. "Why?"

"I'm wooing you for Valentine's Day."

"*Wooing* me? Are you from the middle ages?"

"No, I just..."

"What makes you think I want you to *woo* me?"

"Look, last time we were involved, I was an idiot."

Jenn dabbed at her eyes and nodded emphatically. "Yes. You were."

"Now, after fifteen years, we're both single again."

"We are."

"And, I'm not an idiot anymore. Since I put my foot in my mouth that night your parents came back, I've had a fifteen year case of athlete's tongue. In the freezer, it was like I was standing outside myself watching some moron yell at you, when all I wanted to do was hold you in my arms. That's all I've ever wanted since that night. Don't get me wrong, I loved Melody. Always will."

He took a hitched, shuddering breath. "Jenny, you were my first love. The love of my life. More than anything, I wish we hadn't been apart these last fifteen years."

Jenn's heart swelled.

"So, will you?"

"Will I what?"

"Will you be my valentine?"

"Do you think we can get it right, this time?"

He stood and pulled her to her feet. They were almost hidden from the rest of the room, in the little alcove. And when he took her in his arms, the noise and the movement faded and was gone. It was just them.

He held her gaze with his own. "I *know* we can get it right, this time."

When their lips met, Jenn knew they could, too.

M.D. Posey is the pen name under which author Mark Posey writes romance.

Mark Posey was born and raised in Edmonton, Canada. He has worked as a bartender, a gas jockey, an insurance salesman, a house framer, and a cabinet installer. He also had a ten-year career as a professional wrestler. He toured across Canada on the independent wrestling circuit facing such opponents as The Honky Tonk Man, Dan Severn, The British Bulldog Jr., and NWA World Heavyweight Champion Adam Pearce.

When he's not writing, Mark enjoys cooking, woodworking, watching hockey, and scrolling through social media or taking a nap with his three cats: Pippin, Merry, and Strider.

Mark and his wife, author Tracy Cooper-Posey, currently live in Edmonton. They raised four children: Terry, Matthew, Katherine, and Ashley and now live in their constantly-under-renovations home in Edmonton.

Mark loves to hear from readers so please feel free to contact him at: mark@markposeyauthor.com, or on https://MarkPoseyAuthor.com

Blind Date With
A Hellhound

by Tami Veldura

NARIAH BOYD, BONE WITCH AND leader of the Resistance Against Vampires, was generally not one to accept an invitation to a blind date. And certainly not one on Valentine's day, arguably the worst day to go out to dinner for any reason. Nariah was aromantic, aro for short, and she simply didn't find any of the strappings of courtship to be worth her time. Candle lit dinner was all well-and-good, she wasn't opposed to it, but the idea always seemed to mean a lot more to her friends than to Nariah. It just didn't make her insides warm and fuzzy like people expected.

So it wasn't the Valentine's day trappings that had her fighting for a parking spot in the itty-bitty lot behind Marcelle's, an Italian place that absolutely required a reservation a month in advance. No, she could do without the decorative glittering garland and balloons. The candy hearts were an exception, those were great, and hard to find after the big sale at the end of February.

She snaked into a spot in the front row, her big blue Jeep nosing out two other contenders, and when a vampire hissed at her from the window of her little Sonata, Nariah flipped her off without looking back.

What had convinced her to accept this date—and fight the chaos around it—was, in fact, a detail of Marcelle's itself. You see, Nariah didn't run on much of a budget, and Marcelle's was both out of budget and out of the question. It wasn't even something she could save for an indulgence occasionally. The place was so in-demand, walk-ins were never accepted. You couldn't even get in the front door unless your table was coming up in the next half hour. Nariah had seen photos of the menu online—it changed every week—and there were no prices listed next to the dishes.

And Nariah knew one thing absolutely: If she had to ask the price, she couldn't afford it.

But the thing about Marcelle's that Nariah wanted to see more than the food or the bill at the end, was the singers. Because rumor had it, Marcelle's employed a small staff of Opera singers available on request at any table.

And if Nariah was going to deal with a date, some stranger across the table, and Valentine's Day traffic, she was definitely going to request a song from a trained Opera singer for a personal show.

Nariah was nothing if not practical about the use of her time. She doubted this date would come to anything, but it was worth attending for the chance to enjoy Marcelle's. Even during Valentine's Day. She'd even be able to hold the night over Elidee's head for a good long while to avoid future blind dates. Elidee was a dear, and one of Nariah's closest friends, but she thought romance was life-changing and couldn't help matchmaking everyone she knew. It was occasionally overbearing, but ninety percent of Nariah's social life came through Elidee and they both knew it. The occasional blind date was a small price to pay to not turn into a hermit in two weeks or less. Nariah knew she'd rather spend her time in the local graveyard or processing her latest animal skeleton for armature.

She wasn't called the bone witch for nothing.

But spirits didn't make for engaging conversation, which was at least something Nariah could look forward to tonight. Elidee's matchmaking was never boring, that was for sure. The last three dates had been respectively: a bodybuilding black woman (human, she should add) who did combat training with werewolves, a white nonbinary singer-songwriter who had recently become a hit on the latest social video app and swung through town to hide from their rabid fans, and an actual fairy—a man so beautiful, people of all genders swooned when he walked by. He looked mixed-race, but did the fae have races like humans divided things? Nariah's asexual nature had given her natural immunity to what he called "uncontrollable glamour" but she'd found him too arrogant for her taste, and the night hadn't lasted long enough to find out much about his people. He'd claimed he had wings, but Nariah never got to see them. She still had *so many* questions for him.

Incompatible partners perhaps, but never a dull date when Elidee set them up.

Nariah made the landing just off the parking lot and paused to run a finger across the back sandal strap of one of her flats. It kept flipping up and sitting right on her achilles. She would have swapped them out already, but Nariah's only backup shoes in the car were a pair of bright pink and yellow sneakers for trail-running. Not exactly Marcelle's shoes.

She fixed the strap and fished her phone out of her purse—a black leather bag she wore with a cross-body strap most days. It was one of those bags that seemed bigger on the inside some days, with items that got lost at the bottom if Nariah didn't stay on top of organizing it. It was her daily bag. In fact, it was her only bag—which gave Elidee fits at the very idea—but black leather dressed up or down and Nariah had grown comfortable with its dimensions and weight years ago. Tonight it sat unobtrusively against her dark green knit sweater dress and black leggings. Both meant to keep her warm instead of sexy. She had a softshell jacket draped over her arm just in case she was stuck waiting here on the sidewalk for more than a minute or two. It wasn't cold out, but Nariah shivered anyway. *The spirits had taken her warmth*, her mother had said. Seemed as reasonable as anything else in this world.

Nariah's only concession to the date nature of the night was a pair of gold and emerald earrings that dangled from her lobes. She'd made them herself, wrapping gold wire around and through the very tiny bones of a pair of armatured rat hands. The bone claws each cupped a pair of rough-cut emeralds and, thanks to a touch of magic and moonlight, they held a faintly silver glow.

The glow was incidental. Nariah had charged them with moonlight for higher sensitivity to spiritual energies and the emeralds were a stabilizing influence. Spirits tended to unravel if they weren't firmly bound to their bones. The rat spirit bound to the hands in Nariah's earrings peered up at her from inside the purse before returning to grooming her face and ears.

Phone in hand, Nariah cast a glance across the sidewalk and entrance to Marcelle's. A lot of glittering silver dresses, tasteful black, and spots of pink and red in gift bags, chocolate boxes, and the like. Somehow, the collection of dinner reservations made lingering at the bottom of the steps look like a social war of hierarchy. Look at us, prepared to enter Marcelle's. We're certainly not guarding this spot right at the edge of the red carpeted stairs, but wait a moment, our name will be called next, you'll see.

Nariah addressed her phone. *We need to go shoe shopping.* She texted Elidee. *These sandals have got to go.*

YES. Came Elidee's immediate response. *Outlets, here we come. I've been dying for a shopping trip.*

Nariah snorted. *You just went shopping last weekend.*

Not with you! <3

Flirt.

Only for my favorites…. Don't tell me Varrien has left you hanging. I will call him.

Nariah smiled. *I just parked. Let's give him a second.*

If you're still texting me in 5, I'm calling him.

Nariah chuckled and was still amused at her friend when a low voice called her name as its owner stepped up on to the sidewalk.

"Nariah Boyd?" he asked.

He was tall. Much taller than Nariah had expected. His broad shoulders had been captured in a very nice dark gray suit set off with an emerald green tie. She narrowed her eyes at that. They matched. No doubt Elidee was responsible. Nariah's date outfit was probably not hard to guess at.

This was the kind of thing Nariah didn't understand. What was the attraction to matching? Why was this part of the human-mating-ritual dance? And how gross of a misstep was it that she hadn't thought about it until now?

"Not…Nariah?" The man asked with some hesitation.

Nariah blinked her thoughts and the scowl on her face away. "Sorry." She thrust her hand out to cover the social stumble. Man, she was just firing on all cylinders tonight, wasn't she? "Yes, Nariah."

He smiled smoothly, and took her hand. Thankfully he didn't try to kiss it or anything, but the shake he gave was firm and expertly modulated for a man of his size. A practiced shake. The kind of handshake one developed after years of social encounters and business. "Varrien Vicaro."

Nariah lifted both eyebrows. "Quite an evil mastermind name you've got going for you."

His smile widened just a touch and Nariah narrowed her eyes again. That was a measured smile. One meant to be friendly without flashing what hid inside. Elidee wasn't an idiot, she wouldn't set Nariah up with a vampire, which left… "Werewolf?"

Varrien's smile wilted a little at the edges. "I asked Elidee not to tell you so I'd have a chance..."

She didn't blame him. The prejudice against wolves was just as strong as against the vampires, but Nariah didn't hold to it. The wolves hadn't taken over the world. A lot of people treated them like a new and improved AIDS virus, though.

"She didn't. It's not a problem for me." Nariah shrugged, "I've never been on a date with a werewolf but your people tend to avoid mine."

He frowned curiously. "Your people...?"

He'd shown his, so Nariah was willing to show hers. She lifted one hand and indicated the snake-spine bracelet that looped twice around her wrist. She reached for the power inside, a metaphysical muscle like lifting a weight, and asked her companion to manifest. The snake was small, so the weight of the power was small. With a shimmering blue glow, a garter snake slithered out of the bones and onto Nariah's palm. She stretched up a few inches and flicked her ghostly tongue at Varrien.

The werewolf stared and Nariah saw tension crawl across his shoulders and deform the front of his very nice suit. She didn't know enough about suits to identify it, but between the suit, the handshake, the practiced smile— Varrien was a wolf of wealth far beyond Nariah's. She didn't need to know the suit's maker to know it had been tailored for him. He was about to rip the seams of it with the strength of the muscles moving underneath.

"Deathwalker," he finally said, under his breath and with a quiet whisper.

Nariah dismissed her snake friend, who wrapped back into her own bones, and let her hand drop. She eyed Varrien in silence, letting him have a moment to work through whatever he thought he knew.

A series of expressions whipped across his face, starting at aggression and fear, blitzing through confusion, and finally landing on curiosity. He took a deep breath, as though scenting her. Not a human breath, but a huffing one. A wolf movement.

He finally said, "You don't appear to be a demon from hell sent to capture my soul for eternity." His tone was tight, a mixture of seriousness and disbelief.

Nariah blinked. Was that what the wolves thought of her? She knew it was bordering on superstition, but that was a little much from a group largely considered myth until the vampires rose.

"No," she said simply. "Though I haven't met any demons, so I can't say if they're sensitive to spiritual power. If they are, I bet they'd be happy to capture your soul for all eternity." She shrugged, "A dragon once called me a Bone Witch. That's the title I prefer."

"A dragon," he said flatly.

From the top of the stairs, a clear voice called, "Vicaro, party of two? Vicaro?"

They both broke away to look up the red-carpeted stairs, then back to each other.

Varrien made a slight gesture toward Marcelle's. "May I take you to dinner, Nariah? Perhaps we both can learn a little about each other."

"I would like that," she said.

VARRIEN WAS IN THE MIDDLE of laughing uproariously over the coffee-and-dessert course of a pair of creme brulee — with the sugar coating bruleed right in front of them at the edge of the table — when Nariah's emerald earrings flared with blue light.

Nariah had learned a lot about wolves, or at least this wolf in particular. He let every emotion cross his face without censure and he indulged in each of them wholly. Laughter was bellyaching, surprise was complete astonishment, and the like. He threatened to be overwhelming, but each time Nariah started to feel hemmed in by his boisterousness he seemed to sense it. Varrien regularly turned the conversation back to her, and expertly quieted himself to listen—nodding and mmhmm-ing in all the right places.

So the dinner passed easily and Nariah found herself surprised to have enjoyed it by the time dessert came to the table. She liked Varrien. He was big, both physically and emotionally, and yet held a level of social intelligence Nariah found lacking in most people. Like that fae she'd had half a date with.

So when the earrings flared with light, washing out her vision and pulling startled sounds from all the tables around them, Nariah felt her gut fall in disappointment. She didn't want the night to end yet.

The rat spirit riding around in her purse sprung from the black bag and hooked her ghostly claws on Nariah's sweater dress. She clambered swiftly upward, gaining the table and stretching her nose up into the air until she stood on her back legs. Sniffing and sniffing and sniffing. Nariah hadn't called her onto the mortal plane, but the strangled sound in Varrien's throat said he could see her.

Nariah reached for the power swirling in her earrings and drew it carefully inside. The light dimmed. Nariah blinked the spots away and realized several people had paused in their meals to stare at her.

Before she could apologize, or even think of a reason why the power would flare like that, shaking hit the entire restaurant. It started in the champagne glasses, tinkling as they vibrated against each other on the racks and tables. Then the dishes began to rattle on their chargers and people lifted their hands away from the tables in alarm.

Varrien shot to his feet, Nariah right after him. She scooped the rat spirit up with one hand and dropped her on her shoulder instead.

Then the shaking really hit. An earthquake that rattled the windows in their walls and tipped soup out of bowls. The earth dipped like a wave on the ocean. Nariah spread her feet and held on to the table.

A woman screamed in surprise and fell, taking the tablecloth, the dinner service, and every drink with her. Her date rushed to help her back to her feet.

"EVERYONE STAY CALM," Varrien barked suddenly, his voice carrying clearly through the room and drawing all the attention. His size and stature helped command the space and he looked around, meeting eyes with practiced confidence. He pointed toward the front door. "Gather your party and walk to your cars. Move away from the building."

People blinked at him.

Nariah turned to the closest table where a woman in an elegant red evening gown sat, staring with alarm at the wine jumping in its glass. She grabbed the woman's elbow firmly and held it through her startled jump and tug away. "Ma'am. Please stand up. Here's your purse." Short sentences and direct instruction were always best in an emergency. The woman took her bag automatically, the way people tend to do without thought when you hand them something.

Nariah gestured at her date, an older white man in a light gray suit. He was balding. "Sir, right this way."

She put the woman's hand in his and gave them a push toward the door.

That seemed to unlock everyone else. People stood all at once, voices rising in alarm and confusion. Bags were found, elbows were held, people turned and helped their neighbors untangle from tablecloths and napkins.

The earth rolled and threw people. Shouts of alarm and pain clustered at the doorway. Then the Marcelle's staff entered from the kitchen all in a wave of white and black, on hand to help people stand and direct the crowd down the stairs and away from the building.

Nariah snatched her bag from the chair and slung it over her shoulder securely. The ground rolled. She grabbed Varrien's arm as he helped an elderly woman with her walker and he managed to hold them all up. Then together, they made for the front door.

Spirit power flexed inside Nariah's chest with the force of a sucker punch. She gasped, one hand on her chest as the other groped for the door jam. Her vision tunneled for an alarming moment.

She felt an overwhelming urge to run. To hunt. To *feast*. She needed to feel the power of a spirit as it dissolved on her tongue and teeth.

Then her vision popped back into place like a bubble and the feasting urge was gone as quickly as it had come.

The rat on her shoulder poofed her fur up in alarm. Nariah felt it along her skin like goosebumps. "Yeah," she agreed. "No kidding."

Whatever she'd sensed was on the hunt and Nariah had no doubt the earthquakes were related.

"Nariah!" Varrien took the red-clad steps three at a time to come back for her.

She pushed off the doorway and met him half way. "There's something spiritual going on. I need to track it down. I'm sorry to cut our date short—"

He waved that away with a sharp gesture. "The date can wait. How can I help?"

He surprised her with his earnest willingness and Nariah stumbled over her thoughts for a moment. "Er... help?" Could he help? She wasn't used to working with anyone—not since she was young anyway—and she didn't know what capabilities a werewolf had in the spiritual. She was willing to bet he was great to have as backup in a fight, though.

"Hold on," she said, and made a small circle with her arms. She held her own hands in front of her at shoulder height. "Where is it, Rena?"

The rat spirit scrambled confidently down Nariah's shoulder, across her elbow and paused at her right wrist. She backed up a few steps, then pointed her nose outward about 1 o'clock. Nariah looked up across the parking lot. Varrien turned to do the same.

Marcelle's parking lot was tiny, as befitting its elevated branding, and unlike nearly every other block in downtown, they didn't have to share it with other buildings. Instead, there were a series of landscaped dividers along the sidewalk and at the far end of the block, a walkable park. In the center of that park stood an old brick clocktower that pre-dated the vampire Rise.

Rena's nose pointed firmly to the right of that clock tower, across the two-lane street with metered parking, and directly at the dark, square building of a bank. Some kind of credit union with a ticker on the side to show the temperature and time.

The ground rumbled again, quieter and with less flowing. But then a heartbeat later, a massive fireball soared up from behind the bank across the street and crashed in glittering firework fashion against the brick clock tower on this side. Fire fell in dripping cascades onto the lawn and manicured bushes, lighting secondary fires instantly.

People in the parking lot gasped. Many ducked in surprise.

Nariah and Varrien took off running down the stairs and out onto the street toward the bank.

"What is it?" Varrien called as they made the corner of the street and picked up speed.

"No idea!"

"What do we do about it?"

Nariah huffed a laugh between gasps. "Also no idea!"

The closer they got, the brighter Nariah's earrings began to glow, until, at the bank, their light started to interfere with Nariah's vision.

Varrien reached the bank corner first and pivoted out into the drive-through lane without hesitation. He jerked and threw himself back behind the wall of the bank only inches before a fireball the size of a sedan roared through the air and engulfed a city tree planted in the sidewalk.

The tree wasn't what Nariah would call "flourishing," but it went up in spectral flames like it had been dead kindling for ten years, a *whoosh* of fire that made her stagger to a stop and put a hand up to protect her face.

The light in her earrings dimmed.

Varrien shot her a curious glance. "You do this often?"

"Ah?" Nariah toggled her hand in a so-so gesture. "Enough," she said. "The fire's new. Did you see what it looked like?"

"Not well. Small or low to the ground. It's under the drive through cover of the bank ATM just around the corner, close to the wall."

Nariah stared blankly at the burning tree, thinking hard. "Small, but can throw fireballs. Enough spiritual power to cause earthquakes...." She shook her head. "I have no idea. Not harpies, not vampires, but that doesn't narrow it down much."

"Not werewolves," Varrien added.

She acknowledged with a nod. "Ok, sit tight. I'm going to feel it out and see what we learn. If it comes running around the corner, let me know."

"Do you expect it to come running around the corner?" He asked, his voice rising a little in alarm.

She shrugged. "I'm going to do the spiritual equivalent of giving it a poke. It might not like that."

He nodded, then faced the corner and spread his stance like he was about to have a wrestling match. The dress slacks weren't made for that kind of stress and they strained around Varrien's truly massive thighs.

Nariah closed her eyes. She reached for the power in her chest. Usually it took some concentration, a little lifting to push it out, but whatever was on the other side of the bank wall seemed to be dumping power into the area like a fire hose. It all but leapt into Nariah's metaphysical hands when she called for it.

In a pulse not unlike sonar, she thrust it back out and listened for the echo. She was expecting a spiritual bounce, but the power of the thing swamped her ping entirely.

Instead, she heard the yelp of a very small dog.

She snapped her eyes open.

Varrien had straightened in surprise. They traded a look, then leaned around the corner cautiously.

No fireballs tried to take off their faces.

Another yelp, this one sounding even smaller and more pathetic. Followed by a series of whimpering whines.

"It's...a chihuahua?" Varrien asked with deep confusion.

Before Nariah could warn him that it probably was not a normal dog, he jogged around the corner. She startled after him.

The bank was old brick, darkened by weather and time, and streaked with water stains on either side of the drive-through shelter. The magical chihuahua huddled against the brick in the muck of the edge of the wall and pavement. It looked like a normal dog, small, with oversized ears, and shivering to death as it curled up even tighter in a ball. Its light fur was streaked with soot and mud, it's paws looking like they'd been dipped in brown paint.

Varrien approached.

Nariah hesitated. The spiritual pressure coming off the dog was alarmingly large. Mastiff-sized power. Small bear sized. Either it wasn't what it appeared to be, or something was riding the dog. Like a hijacker from another realm—only instead of a car, the vehicle was this chihuahua.

Varrien crouched as he moved closer, only ten or so feet away. His voice softened and he extended one hand, crooning.

The chihuahua bared its teeth and cowered. Not an agressive sign, but a fearful one. The thing had its big ears tucked flat on its tiny head and its little stick of a tail quivered against its belly, tucked up between its legs. It licked its lips and the eyes too big for its head rolled, showing white.

Varrien paused.

For a moment the two of them remained like that, Varrien beseeching and the dog a quivering ball of terror. He seemed to understand that pushing closer would lead to a fear bite.

The change came slowly, and only in the spiritual. Nariah kept her senses open, spread wide to watch the metaphysical in the same way Varrien watched the dog. It felt like a predator and she knew better than to take her magical eyes off the ball.

So when the power began to curl in on itself, condense like water in a cup, she noticed. It felt like the big bad wolf was shrinking at first, the wide edges of it collapsing inward. But the power didn't weaken. If anything it became more potent. Like reducing a sauce over low heat. Stronger.

Ready to explode.

Her earrings flashed.

Nariah lunged for Varrien the moment she realized what that power was preparing for. He crouched on one knee before the dog, oblivious to the wind-up happening just beyond his mortal senses. He shifted toward her, the movement or sound cluing him in, and his eyes started to go wide with surprise when Nariah dropped her shoulder and tackled him off his feet.

Her launch threw them to the pavement and they rolled under the crackling, blazing fire that erupted out of the little chihuahua's mouth like a jet engine.

Varrien yelped like a dog, then rolled them both to their feet at a distance. His strong arms kept Nariah upright. Then he growled, a low sound she felt in her back where he pressed against her.

The chihuahua stopped pretending. It still had the form of a small dog, but now it stood confidently on all fours, its entire body a wavering orange and yellow flame. Nariah could almost see through it. The rolling eyes and the mud were both gone, burned away. Only a powerful spirit stood in front of them now, its ears pulled forward, tail straight back, and teeth bared.

"I think we made it mad," Nariah said.

Varrien growled again. Nariah couldn't spare a glance, but she'd bet he was baring his teeth too. Was he going to shift? His hand on her arm was still human...

Nariah dropped her hand to her bag slowly. She'd packed for a date, not a spiritual emergency. "I might be able to banish it...?" she mused more to herself than anything. She kept her eyes firmly on the flaming dog.

The power began to tighten again and so did the light in her earrings. Nariah tensed and Varrien felt it. Together they took a step back, then another, deeper under the drive-through roof.

Varrien squeezed her arm softly. "Say when and we split. You go right, past the wall. I go left."

He was a quick study, recognizing already that Nariah could sense something he couldn't. The only thing to the left was the ATM standing in the middle of the drive-through, but Nariah didn't have time to argue.

The power rolled, tightened.... "Now!" Her earrings flashed with power. Nariah shouted and scrambled to the right. Varrien ducked to the left. A fireball split the air between them and roared harmlessly into the sky.

Nariah tucked herself against the brick wall that made up the far leg of the drive-through overhang. She opened her bag, looking for anything that might help banish a spirit, and scowled at her options. Chapstick, her wallet, a protein bar, a receipt from Target. She fished a bracelet out with an opal woven into it, meant to warn the wearer of vampires in the vicinity, but the stone hadn't been charged. Useless. She threw it back in the bag.

Then the little rat spirit on her shoulder scrambled down Nariah's arm. Rena wasn't a mortal rat. She didn't have to hold on when Nariah ran off down the road or went tumbling to avoid fireballs. She was bound to her bones in Nariah's earrings and couldn't leave their vicinity even if she tried.

Rena perched on Nariah's wrist and put both her hands on the snake-spine bracelet that sat there. She patted the bracelet with both hands, her nose sniffing upward at Nariah, her little eyes focused.

"You think I should bind it?" Nariah turned far enough to peek around the corner at the fire spirit. It stood in the drive-through, blazing like a miniature dog-shaped bonfire. Light and shadow flickered along the brick wildly. "I don't know if that's a good idea."

From his awkward crouch behind the ATM, Varrien scowled at her. "Who are you talking to?"

Nariah made a small gesture with her arm indicating the rat. "Rena. She's a spirit. I needed a consult."

"From a ghost," Varrien said. "Is she magical?"

"No, just dead."

Varrien stared at her for a moment across the empty space of the drive-through. Then said softly, apparently to himself, "This is a very weird conversation."

Nariah shrugged. "You get used to it."

The look he shot her was threaded with curiosity.

Unfortunately Nariah didn't have time to elaborate. The fire spirit turned and began trotting directly away, toward the alley where the drive-through connected back toward the very busy main road.

"No, wait!" Nariah jumped back into the drive-through and ran after it. She swept her hand over the bones of the snake bracelet and hauled on the power around her. There was plenty of it to use with all the fireballs being thrown around.

Varrien pursued her without hesitating. She gave him points for that, even though he had no idea what she was doing. "What's the plan!?" he yelled.

"Nothing smart!" she yelled back. Spiritually, she hauled the weight of power around like a highlander chucking an entire redwood tree across the field. Physically, she flung her hand from the bracelet to the dog and intoned, "By moon and bone I bind thee."

Her voice echoed in the spiritual realm, deeper than normal, and with a pure silver ring around the edges.

Her garter snake spirit, the one she'd shown Varrien earlier that day and had held in the palm of her hand, flew from her bones and inflated to the size of an anaconda in a flash. There was so much power in the air, Nariah hardly had to push.

Her snake hit the ground already slithering around to circle the fire spirit in her ghostly blue coils. The dog growled and tried to bound away, but the snake slapped her tail through the air. The dog plowed into the ground hard enough to ripple the pavement like sand.

Both Varrien and Nariah skidded to a stop with sympathetic winces.

"Oooh, ouch," said Varrien.

The fire spirit sprang back to its feet and barked at the snake. Power condensed.

The snake struck before any fireballs could manifest. Her huge body coiled around and around the little fire dog, squeezing down in rippling waves as she bound the spirit and all of its massive power.

Nariah reached for the magic around her and pulled it out of the air. Her earrings began to glow and Varrien made a concerned sound in his throat. Nariah stretched her arms wide, her fingers splayed as she reached, her face turned up to the sky. The fire spirit had saturated the area and funneling that much power down was like trying to lift a bus. Her muscles bulged as she pulled at it, spinning it into her body and out again as fine thread—condensed and powerful—to the bone bracelet around her wrist. The vertebre began to glow like her earrings, the surface of the bone becoming nearly transparent, like the ghost of the snake herself.

The fire spirit's struggles weakened as Nariah stole the power from the air and fed it to her snake instead. The coils tightened. The snake opened her mouth, massive fangs unfolding from the roof as if to strike.

But she didn't bite the dog. Instead her tail worked out of the tangle of coils and with a final wrench of power, the snake bit herself instead.

Nariah felt the very moment her binding took hold. The knot closed, and with a flicker of blue and red light, both the snake and the fire spirit vanished.

In their place stood a pale chihuahua, its face enclosed in a glowing blue muzzle as it quivered in the crater of the pavement left behind by the fight.

Nariah let her arms fall. She collapsed to her knees, her breath heaving like she'd just run a marathon. Excess power escaped her grasp and swirled back into the air. There was still a lot of it saturating the parking lot, but it would dissipate with time.

Varrien knelt at her side. He reached out, then hesitated with his hands only an inch from her shoulders. His dark eyes were creased with worry. "Nariah? You ok?"

She nodded, but her body gave out and she slumped into Varrien's waiting arms. None of that power had been hers, but she'd funneled it all through her body so fast, she felt like a wrung rag. Empty and scrubbed a little raw on the inside. Her cheek fell to Varrien's shoulder and he held her close. His body radiated heat. Nariah hadn't realized how cold she was.

Then her eyes fluttered closed.

She jerked awake with a gasp and found herself still in the bank lot and still in Varrien's arms. He'd moved them to the curb, so at least they weren't sprawled in the middle of the drive-through. She blinked hard as she tried to swallow the cotton ball in her mouth.

Varrien helped her sit up.

"How long was I out?"

"Only a few minutes. The rat got very distressed at the idea of moving you."

Nariah glanced around and found Rena perched on her knee, seated back on her haunches as she cleaned her face.

The fire spirit, still looking so much like a mortal chihuahua with a glowing blue muzzle, sat with its tail tucked around its feet only an arm-length away. It watched Nariah closely.

Varrien cleared his throat gently. Nariah looked up at him, straightening as she realized she was still leaning into his shoulder. "Sorry."

"Not that I want to dissuade the lady from using me as she needs, but can you explain what happened there? I got lost when you charged in like a bull."

Nariah huffed and smiled a little. She gestured at the dog. "It looks like a chihuahua but it's not actually mortal at all. It's entirely spiritual."

"Like your ghost rat?"

"No, actually," Nariah said thoughtfully. "It's not dead. It's more... elemental. I've never encountered anything like it and I'm not entirely sure it's native to our world. Or maybe not our plane of existence."

Varrien hummed neutrally.

"I was going to banish it," she continued. "But Rena suggested I bind it instead."

"And you listened? To the rat?"

Nariah ignored the note of disbelief and treated the question on its face. "Well I don't have my kit, it's in the Jeep. So, she was right, a binding was the better option."

Varrien nodded at Nariah's wrist, where her snake-spine bracelet glowed so blue it was translucent. Just like the muzzle on the dog. "And that's where the snake came in."

She turned to look at him again. "How much do you know about spirits?"

"You're the first deathwalker I've spoken to at any length."

"Yeah," Nariah said casually. "Still think I prefer bone witch instead." She lifted her wrist, indicating the bracelet. "Spirits are very flexible things. They can behave in metaphorical ways. Animals are better at this than humans. People can't conceive of being anything other than the person they are, but a snake…. Well, my snake specifically. She had dreams of grandeur. She's thrilled that I can fill her with power and make her larger. And she's very good at tying things up."

They both looked at the chihuahua who dropped its ears back and growled in return. The effect was lessened considerably by the lack of fireballs.

"So why hasn't it run off?"

"Spirits are tied to their bones. They can choose to release that binding and move on from the world, but not all of them are ready to go yet. That's probably as far as my snake can get, so it's like putting the dog on a leash."

Nariah pushed herself to her feet and took a few steps back experimentally. The dog swung its head toward her—or perhaps the muzzle dragged it—and though it obviously resisted being pulled, it trotted after.

"So now I've got a leashed elemental, I guess," she said. "Do we know where those earthquakes started? I want to see if I can put this thing back where it came from."

Varrien stood as he jerked his chin across the neighboring alley and toward the next block. "Not far that way. The sirens have been stopping short of Main."

Nariah frowned at the empty alley and the office building beyond. "You can tell that from here?"

"Werewolf," he said.

"Oh, right. Handy."

They walked.

Nariah kept an eye on the chihuahua as they made it to the sidewalk and turned toward flashing cop lights. She was worried it might fight the binding or even get free. She didn't have enough juice to bind it a second time. But even though it flattened its ears and growled at her every time she glanced over, it trotted after her like a well-trained hound without any trouble.

Varrien cleared his throat with obvious nerves. "Um. This is abrupt, but, would you like to get coffee later this week? Maybe Friday?"

Nariah gave him a curious look. "Sure? Why?" She didn't mean for her tone to be suspicious, but it came out a little hard.

Varrien blushed. Nariah watched the red climb up his neck in fascination. She'd clearly missed something.

"Er…" He glanced at her, then forward again deliberately. "I'm asking you out."

"Oh," Nariah blinked. "*OH, shit.*"

He stopped on the sidewalk and turned to her with a heavy crease between his brows. "Did you forget we were on a date?"

Nariah stared at him, refusing to break eye-contact even as her own blush started creeping up her cheeks.

Varrien snorted. Then he laughed, the bark of it startling and loud as he guffawed and held his stomach. "Oh, oh, my god. You forgot."

Nariah mock-scowled. "In my defense, this is not the normal sequence of date events! I got distracted!"

It took a moment for Varrien to catch his breath, and he was still chuckling when he said, "I get the impression this is exactly the normal sequence of date events with you."

Nariah turned on her heel, marching toward the flashing lights at the end of the block. Varrien kept pace with his long legs, still smiling to himself. She scrunched her nose. "Then why do you want to do coffee?"

"Because this is the most interesting night I've had in months," he said simply.

Nariah was silent for a moment. Finally she said, "I don't like coffee." Then she realized that sounded like a rejection of the idea and followed up with, "So let's go to Bean & Leaf. I can have tea."

"Deal. Friday?"

Nariah pulled her phone out of her bag and flicked through her calendar. "I have a morning client. How's one o'clock."

"Done," he said promptly.

Nariah shook her head. People who kept their schedules in their heads accurately were aliens, she was sure. She dropped the phone back in her bag.

Maybe werewolves were aliens. She gave him a curious look. Wouldn't be the weirdest second date she'd ever had. With a shrug, she nodded, and focused ahead. They'd arrived at the cop cars.

Varrien stepped in front of her. Not entirely. And not deliberately, she thought, but forward and head up, shoulders back, eyes narrowed at the milling cops holding off curious onlookers.

A building had partially collapsed. It was an old, stone structure on the corner of the block, formerly a city building of some kind that had wide stairs leading up to the door and several columns holding up the triangle face of the entablature above. The colonnade had collapsed into chunks across the stairs and the entire roof tilted alarmingly to one side. A very large hole in the side, rock spilling like a gutted game animal into the street, gaped large enough to see not only the ground floor but the second story offices as well.

And the swirling portal of red and yellow fire that burned merrily in the middle of the second floor.

"Ah," said Nariah. "I wonder who cut a hole in reality."

"I smell vampires," Varrien growled.

"It is past sunset." Nariah stepped up next to Varrien where he'd paused at the edge of the sidewalk. She straightened her shoulders and projected her voice clearly toward the building. "Magnolia Kiss, I'm here to return your fire elemental."

Several cops turned to look at them. Two started to approach, but they froze a moment later when, instead, a vampire flickered into place in the road. His speed so incredible he appeared to teleport into place. He was black, or had been before being turned, so while his skin tone was lighter than it had been in life, it was still much darker than your average undead. He wore a gray suit—not, Nariah noticed, as nice as Varrien's—and held his hands behind his back. His head, bald, tilted in greeting to Nariah. He didn't acknowledge Varrien.

Nariah felt the werewolf bristle next to her and spoke before something unfortunate could happen. "Darius," she said by way of greeting.

"Nariah," he replied. "It's always lovely to see you."

"I can't say the feeling is mutual." Her voice flattened. She made a slight gesture downward at the dog. "Did you lose something?"

"Bringing me gifts on Valentine's day, are you? I knew you'd come back to me."

Varrien audibly growled. The hair stood up on Nariah's arms and she scowled. She'd dated Darius once, a long, long time ago. Back when he'd been human and they'd both been in high school. Back before the Rise of the vampires. She'd broken up with him just before he was turned and she honestly wasn't sure if he remembered that.

"Oh yes," she said, her words dry. "All you have to do is pick it up."

Darius didn't move, unfortunately. He narrowed his yellow eyes at her and offered a halfhearted smile without fangs.

Nariah wondered if she'd have the guts to burn Darius alive if he gave her the chance. He certainly deserved it, but she paid her monthly tithe to the Magnolia Kiss for their protection and Darius wasn't high enough in the vampire food-chain for his death to make much of an impact on the group.

It would be personally satisfying, though.

Too bad he turned away and said, "Follow me."

Maybe next time.

She took a step forward. Varrien grabbed her arm.

He was gentle about it, and released her the second she paused to turn to him with narrowed eyes, but Nariah could tell by the swell of his shoulders and dark glower on his face that he wanted to do more. Like pick her up and run off to protect her from the vampires. He got points for restraint.

"I don't think this is a good idea," he finally snarled.

She didn't take the anger personally. It was probably vampire-related. She felt the same. "This is where we part for the night," she said as gently as she could.

Varrien looked down at her with surprise. Then his face shuttered, hiding anything else he might be feeling. He glanced up at Darius' retreating back, then down again to Narriah. His lips pressed tight for a moment. "Aren't you the le—"

"What I am is returning a fire elemental to vampires while they listen in on this conversation."

Varrien snapped his mouth shut and had the grace to blush. He nodded once, acknowledgment and apology. Then he took a deep breath and let it out. "Alright. Thank you for a very interesting night, Nariah. I will see you Friday?"

She nodded, holding eye-contact even though it made her skin crawl right up her throat. She didn't want him to think she needed saving. "Friday," she confirmed.

He didn't move. Nariah stared him down, her eyebrows slowly lifting until he finally blurted, "Can I give you my number?"

She smiled. "Let's see how Friday goes. I'll text Elidee when I get home tonight."

He didn't like that. She could see him chewing over the idea and looking for a reasonable excuse to insist. His protective instinct was strong and she watched him fight it.

"Good night, Varrien," she said, her voice touched with finality.

His shoulders slumped a little. "Good night, Nariah."

She didn't like the kicked-puppy look he gave her as he turned away, but she didn't let it make her feel guilty. She didn't know much about him yet. He was an interesting conversationalist and not overbearing, but throwing him into the vampire Kiss when he very obviously couldn't stand them was asking for disaster.

She turned away and approached the destroyed city building. Darius waited for her at the alley corner and led her into a side door still intact. With little clicking claws, the chihuahua followed, dragged along by the muzzle.

Darius led her up two flights of stairs where the earthquakes and whatever had summoned this portal had done a number on the offices. Several desks were piled up in one corner, looking like they'd been flung there with force, their chairs atangle among them. The immediate space of the portal had been cleared when it manifested, eating through wood, stone, and metal that might have been in the way. Half a desk still sat beside the edge of it, it's other half perfectly intact, just on the other side of swirling fire.

A woman in an elaborate clockwork wheelchair dotted with glowing runes sat before the portal, her arms held out before her as she wove a tangled spell with her fingers. Nariah knew the woman well. She had her white hair pulled back into a tail to keep it out of her face, and she wore a familiar white lab coat over her blouse that had been tailored short for the wheelchair. Anesa had run a small occult shop downtown for years before the Rise and still ran it now, catering to a more eclectic customer base.

Darius stepped to the side and allowed Nariah to approach.

Nariah came up to the wheelchair and faced the portal. It was a good ten feet away, but the power of its fire heated her face uncomfortably. She addressed the artificer. "Anesa. They got you over here fast."

She didn't speak for a moment, the spell-weaving taking all of her focus. With a final spread of her fingers, blue magic, like flowing water, cascaded over the portal in a waterfall. The heat cut off suddenly and Nariah hummed her appreciation. The cage of power spun counter clockwise to the portal's spinning fire and contained it.

Anesa let her arms drop with a sigh. "I felt the thing open up and was on my way by the time to vampires took control of the building." She looked at Nariah, then down at the dog. She noted the muzzle. "Oh! Is that the one that got out?"

"I bound it in the bank parking lot. You only lost one? I haven't felt any others."

"Just the one that I saw."

Nariah indicated the water barrier. "Can I throw this thing back in, then? Or do you need to take that down?" She didn't want Anesa to have to re-do her work, but

Nariah couldn't have a fire elemental tailing her all night either.

Anesa considered the chihuahua. "Should be able to pass through from this side, it just can't get out from the portal end."

"Perfect," said Nariah. She passed her hand over her snake-bone bracelet and once again lifted that weight of spiritual power.

Like in the parking lot, the power here saturated the air. The portal was the source, pushing it out in waves like an incoming tide. It was weirdly easy to call on, and the muzzle around the chihuahua glowed bright, brighter, before all of a sudden it was a snake again, wrapped around the flaming body of a mostly-dog-shaped elemental.

"Throw it in, Sin," she said.

The snake flicked her tongue at Nariah for shortening her name, but the snake had chosen something with five syllables and half of them were S's. Nariah avoided trying to pronounce it when possible.

Still, the snake didn't want to hold on to a flaming ball of anger, either, so she pivoted, unrolling her coils so that the dog slid up into the curve of the end of her tail. She whipped her tail around and launched the thing right into the center of the portal.

The water barrier rippled like a stone had been dropped. The elemental barked twice, the sound clear at first, then muffled by water, then cut off abruptly as it flew back into its own dimension.

Nariah cycled her power, releasing it gently back into the world so that it settled neutrally into the ebbs and flows of the natural eddies. The portal was doing a lot to mess with that, though.

"Do we know what this is yet?"

"I heard someone call the dog a hellhound," Anesa said. "But I don't think hell is on the other side. More like an elemental plane."

Nariah gave a sidelong glance to Darius. He'd been unusually quiet for this exchange and she found that suspicious. He raised an eyebrow at her.

She shook her head and put a hand on Anesa's shoulder. "I need to get going. I was on a date—"

"On Valentine's day?" Anesa looked up at her in surprise.

Nariah held up a hand. "I know. But Elidee set it up and the guy made reservations at Marcelle's."

That made Anesa's eyebrows go up. "I'm sorry a hellhound crashed your date."

"He was surprisingly cool with it," Nariah said smiling, remembering Varrien's willingness to engage at the bank. "He gets another shot on Friday."

She gave Anesa's shoulder a squeeze before any questions could work their way out. "Thanks for getting this mess under control. G'night."

"Night," Anesa said lightly.

Nariah followed Darius back down the stairs where he escorted her to the edge of the police line. She very nearly got away without having to speak to him when he said too casually. "So. Varrien Vicaro."

Nariah couldn't stop herself from rolling her eyes. "Having me followed, Darius? Or stalking me yourself?"

"Stalking you? Because I recognize Varrien? Son of bank magnate Archebald Varrien, billionaire and alpha werewolf of the entire western United States?"

Nariah blinked and hoped her face remained as blank as her brain. It seemed lovely "just want a date night" Varrien had some more explaining to do.

She turned away from Darius without a word and began walking. She'd ended up a few blocks from her car and it was already late.

"Don't get caught up with him, Nariah! He's trouble!"

Nariah yelled back without turning around. "You gave up any right to dictate my love life when you cheated on me and I dumped you, Darius! In high school!"

"I'm telling you, he'll drag you into some shit!"

"Good night, Darius!"

Thankfully, whatever tasks occupied him at the building with the fire portal kept him from coming after her. Nariah marched for her car, but not without pulling out her phone to Google Varrien and confirm Darius wasn't blowing smoke. She scowled at the thousands of hits she got on the family name and tabbed over to her texts.

She typed to Elidee, *Date is done, we need to talk.*

What do you think? Good for a second?? Elidee replied immediately, like she'd been waiting with her phone in hand.

Nariah found her Jeep where she'd left it, front row at a now-closed Marcelle's and climbed in as she called Elidee and put her on the Jeep's speakers.

"Was the food amazing?" Elidee squealed as a greeting.

"It was," Nariah admitted. "But I never got that opera singer personal show."

Elidee picked up on Nariah's hard tone immediately, her voice dropping. "Oh, no. Tell me everything."

TAMI VELDURA IS AN enby/aro/ace author of queer fiction. They have published short stories in anthologies *Fresh Starts, Hauntings, Love Among The Thorns, Love Is Like A Box Of Chocolates, Street Magic* (a Diamond Quill Book Of The Year winner), the magazine *Galaxy's Edge*, and they are a contributing member of the scifi magazine *Boundary Shock Quarterly*. They publish new work every month, crossing every genre, but always featuring queer characters and found families.

Tami's stories often feature a motley crew or an underdog, they often write about chosen family, and even if it's scifi, they always try to squeeze a dragon in.

Find out more about Tami at https://tamiveldura.com/ and for more fiction featuring the Bone Witch, see https://books2read.com/u/m2dvKk.

Did you enjoy this anthology?

How to make a big difference!

Reviews are *powerful*.

Authors and publishers like us, without the financial muscle of a sleek New York publisher backing us, can't take advertisements out in the subways and billboards of the world.

Honest reviews of our books help bring them to the attention of other readers. If you enjoyed this anthology we would be grateful if you could spend just a few minutes leaving a review (it can be as short as you like) on the book's page where you bought it.

Thank you so much!

The Authors and Stories Rule Press

This is a Stories Rule Press title

https://StoriesRulePress.com